'The ring's lo[n...]

'I know that. If it ever does get w[ashed...] the river I know it will be miles from here.' Clancy bit her lip, recalling ruefully, "It was a bit loose, and Hugh wanted it made a better fit, but I wouldn't take it off.'

She had been so sure that she would never be parted from her ring as long as she lived. 'In a million years nobody would expect me to throw it away,' she said. It had been the last thing she had expected herself.

Fergus burst out laughing. 'It was quite a gesture.'

He could laugh. While she was here the ring-dumping seemed so crazy that it was comic. When she got home it would be a very serious matter. But with Fergus, where a little madness didn't go amiss, it was easy to laugh.

Jane Donnelly began earning her living as a teenage reporter. After she married the editor of the newspaper, she freelanced for women's magazines for a while, and wrote her first Mills & Boon® romance as a hard-up single parent. Now she lives in a roses-around-the-door cottage near Stratford-upon-Avon, with her daughter, four dogs and assorted rescued animals. Besides writing, she enjoys travelling, swimming, walking and the company of friends.

Recent titles by the same author:

A VERY PRIVATE MAN

FIANCÉ FOR REAL

BY

JANE DONNELLY

MILLS & BOON®

First published in Great Britain 2000
Harlequin Mills & Boon Limited,
Eton House, 18-24 Paradise Road, Richmond, Surrey TW9 1SR

© Jane Donnelly 2000

ISBN 0 263 82092 0

Set in Times Roman 10½ on 12 pt.
02-0008-50513

Printed and bound in Spain
by Litografia Rosés, S.A., Barcelona

CHAPTER ONE

CLANCY LINDHURST leaned over the stone wall and looked down into the fast-flowing river. Then she took off the diamond and amethyst ring, opening her fingers wide, letting it slide from her hand so that it dropped into the rushing water.

She leaned over further, although there was no chance of watching it go; the river was too deep and too fast. But there was something fascinating in the patterns of swirling eddies, and the river sounds made a strange hypnotic music. She stretched down until her fingertips were almost touching the surface, and she could feel the spray on her face when suddenly, without any warning, a hand gripped her shoulder, startling her off-balance, pitching her over the low slippery wall. She screamed as the waters closed over her.

It was like plunging into ice. The cold paralysed her. Her coat and shoes were heavy and the currents were whirling her around, filling her nose and mouth and lungs as dragging weeds trailed around her legs.

But then something was pulling her up again, until her face broke the surface. She panicked, gulping for air, struggling wildly even when there was grass and shingle beneath her. Still choking, water gushing from her mouth and nose, forced out of her, she began to heave, breathing in great shuddering gasps.

When she opened her eyes she was lying on her stomach, her head turned, and the first thing she saw was the shaggy head of a great black dog. The animal's hot breath made her gag again. It was an ugly brute, something out of a nightmare.

So was the man, leaning over her, his hands still on her. Shaggy black hair fell over his face. He was unshaven and he was glaring. He had pushed her in; he had to be crazy, 'Get away from me,' she croaked.

'Save your breath,' he panted. 'Can you stand?'

It was all she could do to get to her knees, but he was hauling her up and everything was whirling around her. She had never fainted in her life but she was going to faint now, and as she became a dead weight and slumped to the ground she heard him cursing her.

She hadn't the strength to speak as she was half carried, stumbling, up the steep winding path to the little hotel, and the man who was dragging her along said nothing. If he had left her she would have stayed where she fell and got hypothermia at least, soaked to the skin in this cold before she could reach her van. She was too exhausted even to crawl.

As they reached the building, and he let go of her to open a door, she found herself sliding down a wall, blacking out again. When she opened her eyes this time she saw a stove, glowing red behind bars. Some time the warmth must reach her. It hadn't yet, but it would if she lay quietly here until she was up to taking off her sodden coat and the shoes that weighed like lead.

Somebody was taking off her shoes. She guessed it was the man; it wasn't likely to be the dog. And he was lifting her enough to drag her arms through her coat-sleeves.

'Drink this,' he said. He held a glass out to her and she put up shaking hands to take it. Whisky was not one of her favourite drinks but she made herself swallow. Over the glass she took another look at him, and he *was* worse than the dog. Tall, unkempt, still scowling. 'You look healthy enough,' he said.

'I am.'

'Then there's no excuse in the world for what you were doing.'

She had just dropped a very expensive ring in the river, but how did he know that? He sounded as if she was beneath contempt. What was he on about? And then it came to her. From how she had been leaning right over the bridge, reaching down to the water, he must have thought she was throwing *herself* in. His grab had toppled her. It was his fault she had nearly drowned. He was a menace and she wasn't telling him what she was doing here. He could think what he liked; she couldn't care less.

The dog's thick black coat shone wet and sleek and she asked, 'Did he get me out?'

'What do you think?' the man said wearily. 'I shouted fetch?' He was soaking wet himself, dripping a pool of water onto the flagstoned floor, his shirt clinging like a second skin.

Her teeth were chattering. Some of it was the cold, making her shiver uncontrollably and suddenly start sneezing like mad. Mostly it was the trauma of nearly drowning and finding herself with this hellish hound and a man who looked like Heathcliff on a bad night.

'There's a bathroom second door along,' he said. 'Don't use all the hot water and leave the door open. I don't want you going under again.'

She would never get warm until she was out of these wet clothes. She mumbled, 'Thanks,' although she had absolutely nothing to thank him for. Then she got off the sofa. If her legs had given way she would have dragged herself to the bathroom; she could kill for a hot bath.

She reached the door along the passage leading from the kitchen and it was a bathroom. Very plain, with white tiles and fittings. Nothing like the pretty little bathroom that had led off their bedroom when she was here before. She shut the door and shot a bolt. She was damned if she was stripping with a door left open and that man just along the corridor.

The central heating was off but the hot tap ran hot and she turned it on full, kneeling beside the bath so that the rising steam warmed her face and hands, staying crouched while she squirmed out of clothes that were sticking to her.

The water was too hot to get into, and she ran cold until the temperature was right, then lowered herself in very slowly, triggering an excruciating rush of pins and needles through her chilled body.

The bathroom upstairs had had a mirrored wall, and in the condensation she had traced a heart and 'C loves H', which had made Hugh smile. That was a silly thing to remember, but so were a host of the memories that were going to haunt her. She wished she didn't have to go back. She wished she could go on running away. But right now she had no strength at all.

She was so weak that when he knocked on the door she could only whimper, and next came a loud rattling of the latch and a shout. 'Are you all right in there?'

'I am *fine*!' That took some effort. 'What do you *want*?'

'Give me your clothes. I'll put them to dry.'

She crawled out of the bath, wrapping herself in the one skimpy towel, and opened the door. He handed her a bigger towel, then began to pick up the clothes she had dropped on the floor. Dripping with water, they looked like dingy wet rags.

He didn't give her another glance. Clutching the towel around her when he went, she wiped the mist from the mirror over the washbasin and found herself staring at a face she hardly recognised. The sparkle in her eyes was quenched. Her dark red hair, flattened out of its usual deep waves, hung limp and lank. I look like a no-hoper who's just been dredged out of a river, she thought. And that shouldn't surprise her because right now that was exactly what she was.

It had begun to rain again, beating against the window pane. She would be an accident waiting to happen if she tried driving through this weather. This was a hotel. Closed. That was displayed on the roadside sign, so the man had to be a caretaker. Or a squatter. Whatever he was there were bedrooms here, and she needed shelter for tonight. Not food. She couldn't face food. But she was at the end of her tether—where a bed was an absolute necessity.

The grey flagstones of the corridor were cold and dank under her bare feet, but she was feverish, and when she got back into the kitchen the air in there seemed stifling. The man had changed into an Aran sweater and dry jeans. His hair looked as if it hadn't seen a comb in days and there was heavy black stubble on his face. He looked tough as a street-fighter and the dog lifted its head and growled.

A nice friendly set-up, Clancy thought with a touch of hysteria. A really welcoming scene. She sat down on the sofa again, the bath towel around her. 'I suppose you want to know—' she began.

She had been going to say something about standing

on the bridge, looking down into the water. That he had startled her, had made her fall, and now she needed a bed for the night, and as it was his fault she was in this state the least he could do was find her one.

But right away he cut her off. 'I don't want to know a thing. You can stay here until your clothes are dry and then I want you gone.' And the brutality of that staggered her. He wasn't even curious why a young healthy woman should be suicidally depressed. He was prepared to chuck her out to try again, and for sheer cold-bloodedness that took some beating. But it did mean she didn't have to invent a reason for being here. Cross-questioning might have caught her off guard, and the last thing she could face was a nosy stranger.

'I need a room,' she said flatly. 'I am going no further today.' She glared back at him, conscious of her nakedness beneath the towel. She could hardly have been more vulnerable but she was desperate.

After a moment he demanded, 'When did you last eat?'

'What? Oh, last night, I suppose.'

She had skipped breakfast except for a quick coffee, intending to get lunch later. She turned her face into a cushion and closed her eyes. She could hear the rain and wondered how she could get through that to fetch her case from the van. She heard the man moving around, and then he said, 'Here.'

He put a tray with a bowl of soup down on the sofa beside her and she shook her head. But she was only weakening herself more by starving herself. When she picked up the tray the towel fell open, but he had turned away and she tucked it around her again.

The first gulps were hard to get down, but she persevered. The soup was thick vegetable and she spooned it in, pausing between swallows because an empty stomach with a residue of river-water had to be queasy. If she threw up on the sofa she wouldn't put it past him to throw her out in the rain.

When she was replacing the almost empty bowl on the tray she could feel his eyes on her, without looking at him. He said, as if it was her fault, 'You're not fit to be driving.' Any fool could see that. 'It's bloody inconvenient, but you'll have to stay the night.'

He was no good Samaritan, and she said scornfully, 'Is that why you got me out of the river? Because you don't want trouble in your neck of the woods?'

'You could be right there.'

'Why don't you want anyone nosing around? Are you on the run?' That was a risky thing to ask, but she was a long way from having all her wits about her yet, and it would be typical of her luck today if she had stumbled on somebody lying low in an empty hotel, a fugitive from heaven knows what.

'I'm not doing much running with this leg,' he said.

He was sitting with one leg stiffly outstretched and she realised that he was disabled. Not seriously, or he couldn't have battled the fast-flowing river and managed to drag her up here, but it couldn't have been easy for him. He could still be in hiding. When she felt better she would worry about that. Right now she felt too ill to care. She said, 'There has to be a bed in a room I can have.'

When he walked across the room he limped, but he was still powerfully threatening, and when he loomed over her, putting a hand on her forehead, she shrank back. She was going hot and cold. Mostly hot. She could feel the sweat trickling from her armpits.

'Great,' he said. 'Just what I need. A gatecrasher with a soaring temperature.'

She had to get into some clothes. Those she had taken off were steaming on a wooden clotheshorse near the stove, nowhere near dry, and she said, 'Please would you fetch my case from my van?'

She hated asking him, especially as it was pouring out there. She would have put on her wet coat and shoes again and gone out herself, but her legs wouldn't have carried her through the rain and she surely couldn't have carried a bulky case.

She had expected him to refuse, and when he went towards the door she said meekly, 'Thank you, I left it—'

'I saw it.'

'It's open.'

'Not much point locking it, was there?' She *hadn't* bothered to lock the van, but he thought that was because she hadn't been planning on coming back from the river.

When he opened the door driving rain came in, splashing the flagstones. Night was beginning to fall, the kitchen was filling with shadows, and in the silence she heard the dog growling again. Like its master, it was allergic to gatecrashers.

'I'm not crazy about you two either,' she told it. But she didn't move a muscle, because she wouldn't have put it past the beast to go for her.

She was almost pleased to see the man again, he could control the dog, but he was only carrying her handbag and the small case that had been on the back seat of the van. He put them on a table, switched on lights, and said, 'There are no rooms heated or beds made, but I can find some blankets.'

'Thank you.' It was warm in here, but she would much prefer an unheated room well away from these two.

'What's in this case?' He was mopping his face with a towel.

'Not much,' she admitted. 'Makeup, chequebook, credit card, a file, a mini-recorder.'

'Any clothes?'

'A pair of briefs and two pairs of tights. There's a bigger case in the boot.'

'Why the hell didn't you say so?' She should have mentioned that; she just hadn't thought. Now he snapped, 'And that's where it's staying. Get into this.' He was holding a shirt that would make a roomy nightshirt. She grabbed it, muttering another thank-you, and pulled it over her head.

When she looked at him again he had an armful of bedding, and she carried her bags, stumbling after him down the passage, to a door next to the bathroom. There was a single bed in there, with a mattress, and two pillows without pillowcases. He dropped the blankets and sheet on the bed and she said, 'Thank you,' again.

'And stop thanking me,' he exploded. 'I am doing none of this out of the goodness of my heart.'

'Have a heart do you?' she heard herself ask.

'I'm sure *you* have,' he said curtly. 'One that rules your head every time.'

Sometimes, not every time and never again. She said, 'You know nothing.'

'Let's keep it that way.'

'Suits me,' she said to the door he had closed behind him. He was a man whose confidences she would not have to share. She had shared too much, in friendship and love, only to find there was no real sharing at all. Just a taking that could drain the life out of you.

The room was spartan as a cell, the only warmth from an overhead light, but it was a bed for the night. She pulled on the pants and the pairs of tights from her little case and then huddled under the blankets. Every bit of her ached, but she had to sleep, because if she was too weak to leave in the morning the man and his dog could be dropping her back into the river.

That was a crazy idea, of course, but the blankets were making her itch and her head was throbbing. She tossed and turned in a troubled slumber from which she kept waking. Remembering, but not believing. Then seeing where she was and knowing what had happened. Going through it again, crying herself back to sleep.

The final nightmare had everything: all the horrors of the day coming together. Rain was still cascading down the dark windowpanes. She watched that, with the wind moaning like a rushing river, and when she fell asleep this time she was drowning again, plummeting to the depths, spinning round and then up, just long enough to see the little bridge.

Hugh was standing on the bridge, watching her as her hands clawed empty air and the weeds dragged her down. Each time she came to the surface he watched her drowning, laughing as she screamed his name.

Mingling with his laughter she could hear a dog barking. There were hands on her and then someone, not Hugh, was saying, 'Wake up. You're all right. It's just a bad dream.'

Her writhing had wrapped the blankets around her, trapping her tight, and her face was wet with tears and sweat. She was as terrified as she had been when it was happening for real, holding onto him, sobbing. 'Where am I?'

'You're safe,' he said. 'You're all right.' He was unravelling the strangling blankets, and as they fell away from her she knew it had only been a bad dream, and for a moment she lay, limp and gasping, against the hardness of his chest.

She was burning up. His skin felt cool to her face, and he pulled the sheet up around her, easing her back onto the pillows, lifting her damp hair from her forehead. 'I'll be back,' he said.

That had to have been the worst nightmare of her entire life. And this had to be the most uncomfortable bed. It was torture to lie on when every nerve in her was screaming. The man had said he would be coming back. He might be bringing her a drink. Her throat was sore. He wouldn't be holding her and telling her she was safe. That had only been while the nightmare lasted, and it had nearly been part of the nightmare.

He came back quickly, switching on the light as he entered the room. Her eyes hurt at first, so that she had to shield them from the dazzle. When she could see he was standing by the bed, holding a glass and a packet.

'Not whisky again,' she protested. It was. With hot water this time, and two capsules that he was tipping out.

He said, 'You're running a temperature. You must know that. If you get away with a chill it's more than you deserve.'

She had been feeling off-colour all morning. Long before she'd gone into the river she had been developing a heavy head cold. 'I can't be ill here,' she wailed.

'Too true you can't. Take the pills and drink the booze and start praying you'll be fit to leave in the morning.' He was wearing jeans, was barefoot and naked to the waist. The stubble looked even darker now; a few more days and it would be a black beard. Not a bad disguise, if that was the idea. Suddenly she couldn't swallow the tablets and she began to cough.

'What's your name?' he asked.

'Clancy Lindhurst. What's yours?'

'Fergus McKenzie. And who is Hugh?'

They had heard her screaming, the man and the dog who had been barking in her dream. The dog was here now, a shadowy shape with gleaming eyes. She said, 'A very good friend of mine I thought I was going to marry.'

'What happened?'

'What do you think happened?' she croaked. 'He dumped me, and don't say you're sorry.'

She knew that was a mistake as the words came out, and he said, 'Why should anyone be sorry for you? Trying to end your life because you were jilted was pathetic.'

She almost said, I was not jumping; but he wouldn't believe her, and what he believed couldn't matter less. She made herself swallow the pills and drain the whisky. He took the glass as she emptied it and said, 'Things could look brighter in the morning.'

'Could they?' She put her head back on the pillow, exhaustion beginning to blur her vision as he switched out the light.

'The rain could stop,' he said, 'although I can't guarantee it.'

In the dark it was a voice you could listen to. 'Sexy' might almost be the word. But there was no sympathy in it. So she had been dumped. No one was going to think that was reason enough for deciding her life had ended. But that was because hardly anyone knew how long she had loved Hugh. His betrayal had almost finished her, so how could anything look better in the morning?

She was sick and totally exhausted, but her thoughts continued to torture her until the drugs and the alcohol closed over her mind and her body and she slipped into a dreamless sleep.

When she woke it was morning. The man was beside her bed again and she groaned, *'No.'* In the grey light of day she was back in a real-life nightmare. She raised herself up from under the blankets and—what was his name? Fergus something?—was handing her a thermometer.

She could have told him she was still feverish, but she stuck it under her tongue and closed her eyes to shut him out. The mercury read a hundred and two and she groaned again.

When he saw it he said, 'You are a very stupid woman,' and she glared up at him.

'We're agreed on that. I'm stupid and I'm sick and you want me out. But you don't want that any more than I do and it is not my fault that I am stuck here.'

'Didn't you realise that suicide can damage your health?'

'Ha, ha.' Her throat was raw but she groaned. 'I could have the flu. I wasn't feeling too bright before I came here. Going into the river didn't help, and I was not jumping when you grabbed me. *You* sent me over that wall.'

That made his scowl even deeper, cutting between the heavy brows. He said, 'You were well over the wall, practically in the water.'

'I was not in the water. I was watching it.'

'Why?'

'Why not?' She couldn't go into details about why she'd thrown away an almost priceless ring. Until she'd let it fall she hadn't realised she was going to do that. She didn't think she was regretting it, although she was going to be told by everyone how stupid she had been. She said, 'It was your fault I went in,' as loud as she could.

'If you say so.' He didn't believe her but he was letting it go. 'Cover up,' he said. 'I'll see what I can find in the first-aid cupboard, and there are probably some heaters around.'

She collapsed back on the bed. 'You were wrong, weren't you?' she said gloomily. 'It didn't get brighter in the morning; it's still raining.' She could see nothing but rain through the window. The long drive up to the hotel ran through the trees alongside the river. If that rose much higher they could be cut off. She felt lousy enough to need a doctor, but nobody knew she was here. She should be telling someone. Not Hugh, but someone. And she asked, 'Can I make a phone call?'

'Sorry, the phone's off.'

If he was the caretaker he'd have the phone. Nobody would be in this isolated hotel without a phone unless they had moved in after it had closed down for the winter months. As he walked with that limp towards the door she called after him, 'What's the matter with your leg? Were you in an accident?'

He didn't look back. He said, 'It was no accident. Luckily he was a bad shot.'

CHAPTER TWO

SATISFIED now? Clancy asked herself. Do you have a death wish or what? Why do you ask these things? If somebody had been gunning for him he was almost surely on the run—and she had to get away from here.

She pushed back the blankets, but as soon as she stood up her legs folded and she slumped down again. She sat there, rocking to and fro as the room rocked round her. She was going nowhere while she was this weak, but a few hours could make all the difference if she could only lie still and keep calm. Stop torturing herself over Hugh and scaring herself wondering if Fergus was as violent as he looked.

That was easier said than done. She was still sitting on the side of the bed when he opened the door a few minutes later. 'What are you doing?' he asked.

'I need the loo. I'll get there. Just let me go slowly.'

Her legs were still the problem. As she reeled into the corridor, much as she had stumbled up from the river, she was in his hands again. At the bathroom door she said, 'I'm all right.'

She did walk in unaided, shut the door and sat on the toilet, her head in her hands. When she ran the tap in the washbasin she managed to wash face and hands, and he opened the bathroom door as she lurched upright.

She walked dizzily back to bed, fell on it and lay with closed eyes until a few minutes later, when he touched her shoulder. Then her eyes shot wide open

and she crawled under the bedclothes. He put a hot
water bottle beside her. There was a one-bar electric
fire and a bucket by the wall, and she croaked, 'What's
that for?'

'It's nearer than the bathroom.'

'I'm not using that.'

'Please yourself.'

A weak giggle rose in her sore throat. 'The final
touch to give this room the jailhouse atmosphere?'

'Uh-huh,' he said, and she could have said, You'd
know about that, would you? Been inside lately? She
didn't, but when he asked, 'Will there be a search
party out for you?' she said something just as stupid,
without stopping to think.

'Not for a few days.'

Now she had made herself even more vulnerable as
a woman alone, and she said quickly, 'Could I possibly have another drink?'

'Sure.'

She couldn't taste this one, but it was hot. Two
more pills. The last two might have helped her sleep
last night, but her throat felt tight and she held these
in the palm of her hand, wondering if she could get
them down.

'Flu and cold relief capsules,' he said. 'Don't flatter
yourself. I'm not drugging you.'

Don't flatter *yourself*, she thought. It would take a
general anaesthetic to put me that far under. She swallowed the pills as he went out of the room, and before
long she was asleep again.

When she woke the bedding was damp, as if per-
spiration had poured out of her, and she felt strangely
light-headed. The heaviness in her limbs had almost
gone. She was not right but she was sure she was

better, and if she had been in her own bed, or any-where she knew she was safe, she could have floated back to sleep again.

But this was no sanctuary. She wouldn't feel safe until she was far away from here, and that shouldn't be beyond her now. She could sit up and move in the bed without the walls spinning. She could stand and the floor stayed steady. She walked slowly across to a chair and the pile of her clothing that had been drying in front of the kitchen stove.

It was stiff from the river-water, but she dressed, managing well enough to boost her confidence. Out of here, she thought, I'll stop where I can get something uncrumpled out of my case so that I look less like a bag lady. Then the first hotel, for a quiet room where I can think quietly.

She was much better. The chill, the touch of flu must have passed the peak, leaving her washed out—and that was a joke almost as weak as she was. But adrenaline was quickening her blood, and she slung the shoulder strap of her purse over her head and picked up her small case.

There were no shoes, no topcoat. Still damp, she supposed, but she often went barefoot. She could reach her van without shoes, and she would rather leave them behind than face the man and the dog again.

She remembered a door from the passage that led to the side of the house. Through that she could reach the car park and, with any luck, get out of the hotel before she was spotted.

She tiptoed from the room, almost giggling because this should be hysterical. Clancy Lindhurst, who prided herself on being in charge of her work and life, had been so wildly out of control for twenty-four hours

that she was now creeping barefoot from a small hotel
like a freeloader dodging the bill.

There were bolts on the door and a key in a lock.
She went at them carefully, making hardly any noise,
but when she stepped outside the building rain came
at her and the door banged behind her.

She began to run, keeping her head down, touching
the side of the house to guide her. And as she heard
the dog barking and the man shouting she fell to her
knees. She was up again at once, sprinting to the car
park. Her Transit van was near the house. She reached
it as he reached her, opened the door and fell in behind
the wheel.

He kept the door open as she rubbed the wetness
from her eyes, but his face was still blurring and she
clutched the wheel and said the obvious, 'I'm going.'

'Into the river again?'

'Just away. That's what you want, isn't it, so why
don't you just let me go?'

'Get out.'

'I will not.'

He grabbed her arm and hauled her bodily from the
van as she spat and struggled. Then he held her upright
and said, 'Look around you.'

'What?'

'Open your eyes, you stupid idiot.' Rain was lashing
her face, blinding her. She blinked hard, still keeping
her head down, and he lifted her chin, turning her head
so that she was looking beyond the man and the van.

A cry that was almost a scream escaped her. 'Oh,
God. Oh, no.'

'Oh, yes,' he said.

The car park was a strip of earth. Beyond that was
a lake. With the rain still coming down, the river must

be overflowing; the track through the trees would be impassable. She couldn't have driven more than a few feet before her car would have been in the water. She would have got out again, it couldn't be that deep just here, but it would have been cold and wet. She was cold and wet already, soaked to the skin again, and so was he, and the idiot dog was frisking around like playtime at the seaside.

She had never fainted before she came here. She had never had hysterics before. But choking laughter was rising in her now, and she had to bite her lower lip to hold it down. Then she turned to get back into the house, stumbling on feet that were too numb to have any feeling through the open door and making for the kitchen and the stove.

She sat hunched on the flagstones before the red glow of the fire, and he followed her in carrying her cases. She was glad to see them. Her lips parted to say thank you, but his expression silenced her until nerves started her chattering. 'Does this happen often, or is it just for me?'

'The river rises in heavy rainfall or snow, but I haven't seen it this bad before. This is serious flooding.'

'Why didn't somebody warn me the wretched place was a trap?'

She was talking nonsense, she knew and he said curtly, 'If you came here to drown yourself what are you whingeing about? Do me a favour. Put suicide on hold. Aggro like this I can do without.' She must have been out of her mind, running barefoot into the rain. She started to sneeze and he said wearily, 'Get back to bed.'

'Can't I stay by the fire?'

'No.'

Her eyes were smarting with weakness and frustration. 'For heaven's sake, why *not*?'

He almost snarled at her. 'Because company is the last thing I'm here for. Much less the company of a neurotic woman.'

She would have disliked him however she had met him. Sitting opposite him in a train she would have had a gut reaction *not* to glance his way. Walking towards him on a crowded pavement she would have dodged rather than brush against him. He was standing still, arms folded, but she got the vibes of furious impatience as clearly as if he had been raging up and down.

She got up from the fire, picked up her small case—her purse was still slung around her neck—and walked out of the kitchen, trying to look dignified and not lurch too much, muttering, 'I shouldn't have thought you'd have had to hide away to be alone. I can't imagine anyone wanting your company.'

The small electric fire had taken some of the chill from the room. She stripped off her wet clothes again and got into bed. She could hear the rain and wondered if it would ever stop, or if the water would go on rising until she was sitting on the roof with the man and the dog, waiting to be rescued by a helicopter team.

He came in with her case and the thermometer, which he handed over. He took that from her before she could read it and said, 'Congratulations, you've notched up another degree.'

She flinched. 'Carry on like this and I could die of natural causes.'

'Not a chance. But don't go walkabout again. Next time I won't be fetching you back.'

There had to be a truce while she was physically dependent on him. He resented her enough for being here; it would be reckless to go on riling him. He was still wet from the rain, and what she had just done was enough to antagonise anyone.

She admitted, 'I was stupid, dashing out like that.'

'Agreed.'

'The rain's got to stop soon, and as soon as I can I'll be on my way. Till then I'll try not to invade your space.'

He almost smiled. 'Let's get you back on your feet, then,' he said.

The service was a long way from tender loving care, but it was adequate. He didn't talk much, and neither did she, but he brought her drinks, refilled hot water bottles. She slept that night, and next morning she ate bread and butter, then at midday an omelette and a portion of tinned rice pudding.

She had a naturally robust constitution and resilience, and by mid-afternoon she was getting dressed again. Not with an eye to another escape bid—the view from the window showed that the hotel seemed to be on a little island, with grey water all around and darker grey skies above—but this time she *was* on the mend, and up to walking around, getting out of this room, breathing some different air.

Out of her case she had taken jeans, a warm sloppy sweater and a pair of black pumps. From the bedroom she turned away from the kitchen, walking down the passage into the public rooms of the hotel.

Closed doors and shuttered windows gave an illusion of shadowy space and her footfalls made no sound on the carpeted floors. It was eerie. So changed in every way from the bustling busy little hotel of her last visit here. In the entrance hall the reception desk was bare. Floral arrangements had gone. Dust sheets shrouded the chintz-covered sofa and armchairs that she remembered.

In the dining room chairs and tables were stacked against the walls, and when she looked across to the alcove where she and Hugh had smiled into each other's eyes and clinked champagne glasses there was no time warp there. Only shadows and silence in a cold and empty room.

She went up the main staircase, reaching the room where she had shared two nights with Hugh. Everything in here had been stripped down for the winter closure, but the four-poster bed still dominated the room and the memory of their passionate love-making, combined with the anguish of her last sight of her lover, in another bed with another woman, was unbearable.

An agony like angina seemed to be tearing her apart, and when the worst of the physical pain began to ease a nerve still throbbed in her head. She should never have come into this room, put herself through this. She had painkillers somewhere in her luggage. She would take a couple and lie down again and zap the headache before it turned into a migraine.

She sat at the bare dressing table in her bedroom downstairs and shook two paracetamols out of an almost empty bottle. Her case was still open on the floor, and somehow the leather-framed portrait of Hugh, that she never travelled without, had surfaced on the top of the contents.

As she gulped on a pill she picked up the photograph, and then the door opened on Fergus. For a moment he stared, then he leapt, grabbing her so that the photograph she was holding went spinning and the pill she was trying to swallow lodged in her throat.

'I can't be watching you every minute,' he roared. 'How many have you taken?'

She couldn't speak for choking, and when he forced her mouth open, making her gag out the pill, she tried to sink her teeth into his fingers. Failing that, she brought her foot back and kicked out as hard as she could, knocking his injured leg from under him.

He howled and reeled back, falling on the bed, going shades paler under the dark stubble of his beard, the string of obscenities through his gritted teeth drowned by her wailing. 'I didn't mean to do that, but it's your fault. I was only taking two for a headache. I am not a suicide risk. I was not overdosing and I was not jumping in the river.'

His breath was ragged. His face was as white as tanned skin could be. He sat very still and he spoke slowly. 'Then why were you doing a high dive over the wall?'

'I was throwing my engagement ring in. I'd stood on that bridge with Hugh. He'd told me we'd be together for ever and suddenly it seemed the right place to get rid of the ring.' She paused, then asked, 'Do you believe me?'

'It sounds crazy enough to be true.'

Like he said, crazy. 'I suppose I shouldn't have done it,' she said ruefully. 'It was a family heirloom. Those were thumping big diamonds.'

Fergus almost laughed, wincing as he did. 'He shouldn't have dumped you, should he?'

'He doesn't know he has.'

'I'm going to be sorry I asked this, but how's that?' She hesitated and he got to his feet, using the bed to haul himself up. 'I'll have to see to this leg,' he groaned. 'You've got a kick like a mule.'

'You had me by the throat,' she pointed out.

'Next thing I'd have been pouring salt and water down you.'

She risked a lighter note. 'There's hospitality.'

'Definitely off season,' he said. 'I was looking in to see if you felt up to sharing a meal.'

After a moment she said, 'All right.'

'See you in the kitchen in ten minutes.' He limped off and she was surprised that her headache had not developed into a blinder. That flash of all-out violence must have released some of her nervous tension, because she didn't seem to be needing a second pill.

She picked up the studio photograph of Hugh and put it away quickly, closing the lid of the case, forcing his face from her mind.

In the kitchen the dog was stretched out in front of the fire and Fergus was sitting at the table, where two places had been laid. 'How's the leg?' she had to ask.

'For a convalescent,' he said, 'your reflexes are dynamite. How's the headache?'

'Much better, thank you.'

'There's no justice.' She smiled when he did. His teeth were white and strong against the dark stubble, although the rate that was growing made him look more of a wild man every time she saw him.

He put a plate with trout cooked in butter and almonds before her, crisp-coated, pink and succulent within. And there was a bottle of white wine. Her appetite was coming back. Another day of healthy eating and she would be almost human again.

As she finished her trout he said, 'Now tell me, how did the engagement end without him knowing?'

They were ships that passed in the night. When she left here the odds were they would never meet again. Suddenly she wanted to talk, and why shouldn't she tell him? She sipped her wine and began, 'Well, I should have been going on a business trip, but while I was driving I started to feel groggy and I wondered whether to turn back. Then I realised I'd left my mobile phone and did go back.'

She kept her voice flat. 'I've got a key to Hugh's house and I let myself in and I went upstairs. He and a girl who I thought was my friend were in the bed I'd got out of that morning.

'They didn't see me. I saw them in a big mirror with a heavy gilt frame that made them look like a painting. His fair hair and her long black hair. Entwined. That's the word. They were entwined. I came away and drove away. I didn't know where I was going. I was supposed to be heading for this gardening exhibition, although I couldn't have gone in if I'd got there, but I just went on driving for hours and then I came to this place. We'd stayed here once.'

She was looking down at her plate but he knew she was seeing the scenes she was describing. 'I saw the "CLOSED" notice but I took the track by the river. I must have been out of my mind, almost thinking I could turn back the clock and it would be like it was.'

She gave a yelp of bitter laughter. 'Of course it was nothing like. The sun was shining then. This time it had been raining for days and there were black clouds and the river was racing under the bridge. I saw nobody around. I left the van and I went down to the bridge. And I remembered all he'd said to me there. Believe me, I never thought of killing myself.' A small shrug. 'But I did drop his ring in.'

She wasn't confiding in a friend. He was almost a stranger. But talking this out had been sharing a secret too heavy to carry alone.

'Did you want it to end?' he asked.

Her reply was spontaneous and heartfelt. 'No, never. From when I was a schoolgirl I had a crush on Hugh. I don't know what I shall do without him. I love him so much.'

Tears were filling her eyes, and when she tried to blink them away she felt them trickle down her cheek. 'I'm sorry.' She couldn't believe she was going to pieces like this. 'You must think I'm an awful idiot.'

'I do,' he said, but his voice was gentle. 'If he matters that much you're an idiot to split over a casual grapple.'

'This wasn't a kiss on the cheek. They were in *bed* together.'

'There's a lot of it about. It rarely means more than a temporary surge of hormones.' His cynicism was probably a typical macho attitude. He went on, 'When you get back you could have it out with them, but I wouldn't take it as proof that the love of your life has dumped you.'

He must never have known how unfaithfulness could hurt, even if it wasn't intended to change anything. Susan couldn't help flirting—she did it all the time. This might have meant no more to either of them beyond a sensual frisson, and Clancy was beginning to feel she would have given years of her life to have known nothing about it.

'Talk to him,' said Fergus.

'How can I?'

'I do have a mobile. I didn't want you giving out the address; this is my bolt-hole. If you want to talk you can, but I suggest keeping the hysterics down. Make it the kind of call he'd expect and see what reaction you get.'

'I don't think I can do that.'

'I'm sure you can.' He topped up her half-full glass, took a mobile from a drawer in the dresser and put it on the table in front of her.

She sipped her way through the wine. Fergus's advice made cynical sense. She would gain nothing by hurling accusations as soon as she heard Hugh's voice, but she needed the steadying kick of the wine. When she picked up the phone and Fergus turned to go she said, 'Please stay. Cut me off if I start screaming.'

He sat down again, facing her as she punched in Hugh's home number. Hugh had a study there, where he sometimes worked, but she got his answer-machine and put down the phone. She was luckier at his main offices, where his long-time secretary, who was old enough to be his mother but still sharp as a needle, put her right through.

There was probably a client sitting the other side of the big mahogany desk, but there was nothing professional in Hugh's manner taking Clancy's call. His voice was warm and intimate; he was delighted to be hearing from her.

'Hello, my darling, I've been waiting to hear from you. Is everything all right?'

'Fine,' she said. 'Everything is fine.'

'When are you coming home?'

'I should be back on Thursday.' Fergus, lounging like a bearded brigand in the chair facing her, was nodding approvingly, and she went on, 'Sorry I haven't rung before. I've been busy.'

'You left your mobile behind. What's your phone number?'

She had left it on his bedside table. If she had stopped at a pay kiosk that morning and rung she might have shattered a raunchy moment. Sharp pain made her catch her breath before she could say, 'I'll phone you. I don't know where I'll be staying.'

'Take care of yourself. I love you,' Hugh said.

'Love you,' she murmured automatically, because that was how they always ended phone calls to each other. She put down the phone, grimacing at the lunacy of this. 'He told me to take care of myself. I wonder what he'd have thought if he'd seen who has been nursing me.'

'So he isn't dumping you?'

'You were right. He didn't count it. It was nothing.' She went on wildly, 'Perhaps it never happened. I was feverish and I didn't see what I thought I saw.'

'Maybe,' he said, neither of them believing this for a second.

'And maybe I'm not marooned here with Bluebeard and the hound of the Baskervilles.'

'We are such stuff as dreams are made on,' he said. 'More wine?' He held up the bottle and she shook her head.

'What I would love is a cup of coffee. Instant would do.'

'You shall have the real thing.'

Those few hypocritical words with Hugh had been an ordeal. She pushed back her chair. 'I'll just freshen up. I need to get my head together.'

He said, 'Sure,' and she went back to her bedroom and sat for a while, thinking.

She had not been dumped. Hugh still wanted to

marry her. Nothing had changed for him. For years Clancy had envied the women in Hugh's life as they came and went, but since he had put that ring on her finger she had believed he was faithful to her.

'Did you want it to end?' Fergus had asked her, and of course she wanted to keep Hugh. But this was a warning that she should take nothing for granted. Clancy had competition, and the way she looked now she would be no contest for any of the willing women.

Usually she was rated a knock-out herself, and the sooner she got back to fighting form the better prepared she would be for facing Hugh on Thursday. She couldn't know what would happen then. It might be wiser to pretend she had seen nothing but she might not be able to carry that off.

Meanwhile she had a little time to rid herself of the drab-haired pasty-faced loser who had been Clancy Lindhurst for the last few days.

Her hair needed washing and conditioning; she would do that later. For a quick treatment she brushed vigorously with sweeping strokes, head down, wincing at tangles, getting to the roots and finally achieving some measure of bounce and shine.

She changed her clothes for a full skirt in caramel-coloured cashmere, matching suede pumps, a soft blue silk shirt and a soft blue cashmere cable sweater, and spent an almost happy ten minutes applying make-up lightly and skilfully.

She was going to need all the confidence that looking good could give her, and she did look good. The dressing table mirror showed her hair as a shining cloud, her skin warm and glowing. Cheekbones and lips touched with coral. Long lashes darkened and a hint of bronze eye shadow complementing the amber flecks in her jade-green eyes.

She was tall and slim with just the right curves, and she smiled, thinking it would be amusing to see Fergus do a double-take when he saw how she usually looked.

None of this was for his benefit, of course, but in the last hour he had been as supportive as a friend.

When she opened the bedroom door the rich aroma of freshly brewed coffee reached her. 'You shall have the real thing,' he had said, and he was as good as his word.

She stood for a moment, framed in the open doorway of the kitchen, and he looked across at her from his seat at the table.

There was silence, during which they both did double-takes and she was as startled as he was. Then they both began to laugh. 'If you want this man of yours, you'll keep him,' Fergus said, and she sat down at the table, never taking her eyes off him.

Then she asked, 'Where did Bluebeard go?'

'Don't tell me you're missing him?'

All he had done was shave, but the change was as dramatic as her own. It was a face as tough as the unshaven man had looked. Perhaps even more dangerous, but stunning. Red-Indian cheekbones, chiselled features, mouth muscles hard.

She said, 'Did you do this because I called you Bluebeard?'

He fingered his jaw. 'You drew my attention to the fact that it was beginning to itch, but Bruno's still brooding about being tagged hound of the Baskervilles.'

Still stretched out in front of the fire, the dog raised its great head and its long tail gave a couple of lazy thumps. There was nothing threatening about Bruno now. He was a big ugly amiable dog.

As Clancy sipped a black coffee from a white mug Fergus asked, 'What do you do for a living?'

'Design gardens. What do you do when you're not—caretaking here?'

He was a journalist, covering the killing fields in a world of manmade and natural catastrophes. When he named places she understood why he would have had no patience with someone he thought was taking her life over a jilting.

'I thought you were a crook,' she confessed as a little silence fell.

'Not far off, but it says "Press" on my passport.'

'And I was sure you were on the run.'

He grinned. 'You're even closer there.'

'Who from?'

'I suppose one good confidence deserves another.'

Elbows on the table and chin cupped in her hands, she waited for what he might tell her in exchange for her tale of heartbreak. She was sure his heart had not been broken, but she was curious to hear more about him.

'Six months ago a colleague of mine was killed,' he said. 'A cameraman. We'd been with the same team for some time and I tried to help his partner. Sorting finances, providing a shoulder to cry on, that kind of thing. What I hadn't reckoned on was her deciding I was Alan's substitute for a whole lot more. She said it was me she'd always fancied, although she wouldn't let herself admit it before, and now there was nothing standing in our way she just knew Alan would be happy for both of us.'

'You weren't happy?' If the girl was ravishing it might have been flattering.

But he said emphatically, 'I was not. It was altogether too slick a move. I thought I was handling the situation, keeping it cool, keeping my distance. And then—this.' He indicated his leg. 'I stopped a sniper's bullet, and the idea of Angela mopping my brow while I convalesced was well off the agenda. So far as she's concerned I'm on a launch floating round the Greek Islands.'

Clancy said gravely, lips twitching, 'Instead of which you're holed up in a shut-down hotel.'

'Legitimately. Friends of mine own this place. It was exactly what I needed. Away from everybody and everything, where I didn't need to see anyone, didn't have to talk to anyone. Marvellous! And then—' he shook his head at her '—I see your van and you on the bridge nearly over the side. And that's what I thought I'd landed. A suicide risk who thought her hard luck was the end of the world.'

'Sorry you got the hard luck tale.'

'I've heard worse.'

That was for sure. She knew pain was waiting for her, but she had to get it into proportion, and being here was like being in another country, where she could almost forget her troubles. Or at least find something else worth talking about. Or even joking about.

She teased, 'Like your own hard luck. How *awful* for you. On the run from a woman who's longing to nurse you back to—?' Mischievously she suggested, 'Virility?' although his lithe muscularity packed a powerfully sexual charge.

'You have a warped sense of humour,' he said.

'Have I? I must try to control it.'

'Why should you? It suits you. Goes with your eyes.'

She laughed. 'When I get out of here I won't believe any of this.' She looked towards the window. 'How long before I get out?'

'It could be another couple of days before a car can get through, but a phone call should get you a ferry.'

Which meant she would be landed somewhere the flash flood had not reached, where she could hire transport and move on, collecting her own van later. She had taken this trip on impulse. A last-minute decision to visit a winter garden exhibition where she would have been busy contacting stallholders whose work she had used in her designer gardens.

She loved her work, but she could not have recovered all her drive and energy, because right now the idea of staying on here was tempting. She had taken a battering; she could be needing a longer healing time.

She picked up the percolator. 'May I?'

'Of course.'

She poured herself more coffee and repeated, 'May I—?' Not stammering exactly although the words came out jerkily. 'I mean—would you mind if I stayed until I can get my van through? I'm not sure I feel too brilliant yet.'

'By all means stay,' he said.

'Thank you,' she said.

And suddenly she had the oddest feeling that something momentous was happening. As though she had turned from the broad highway that was her life and taken a path into woods that were dark and deep with shadows where danger lurked.

CHAPTER THREE

OF COURSE Clancy had not made a life-changing decision. All she was doing was taking a short break. Until Thursday she was pushing her problems to the back of her mind.

Nothing would get her upstairs to that bedroom again, but down here it was as though she had come to this small hotel for the first time and found another guest who was a complex and fascinating man. She could wander around these rooms with no ghosts to haunt her, as if everything was exciting and new.

She indicated a closed door and enquired, 'What's through there?'

'Feel free,' said Fergus.

A larder led off the kitchen, with shelves of tinned and dried food and a well-stocked freezer. Closing the freezer, she said, 'You could last months on this. How long are you planning on staying?'

'A few weeks.'

'Won't you get bored?' She could not imagine him living a hermit's life for long.

'It gives me a chance to catch up on some reading and get on with some writing,' he said. 'Next week I might turn on the radio. Another month and I should be raring to go.'

She looked along the row of tins. She wouldn't think about the last time she was here, nor remember the meals she had shared with Hugh. 'How about soup for supper?' she suggested. 'From this lot I could mix a soup the like of which you have never tasted.'

'You're on,' he said.

That wouldn't take long. In the meanwhile she went into the visitors' lounge and selected a couple of books from a big old-fashioned glass-fronted bookcase. She found a paperback Ed McBain she hadn't read on a lower shelf, and took a Victorian romance from the top shelf.

Shutters were open in here. There was a word processor on a desk, so this was where Fergus worked. She brought her books out. He could have his workroom; she wouldn't be intruding. She started on the paperback, lying on her bed, but after a while there seemed no reason why she shouldn't go back to the kitchen. It was warmer in there, and she could sit quietly on the sofa reading her book.

He was on the sofa, stretched out, all six foot odd of him, arms behind his head and eyes closed. When she opened the door he opened his eyes and said, 'I wondered where you'd got to,' as if he was quite pleased to see her and didn't mind her being around.

She said, 'I found some books.'

'Do you want to know how it ends?' he said, when he saw the paperback.

'Don't you dare. I'll bet you can't tell me how this one ends.'

The old book was bound in faded green, its title, *Cometh Up as a Flower* in gold. There were black and white sketch illustrations of languishing ladies and men with thick moustaches. 'Good choice for a gardener,' said Fergus. 'Ends in tears, probably. Girls in Victorian times who cometh up usually did.'

'What a know-all you are,' said Clancy, and curled into an armchair and went back to her paperback.

Soup for supper was a crab bisque; a tin of crabmeat with tomato soup, pea soup, chicken consommé, cream, and, when all that had been heated slowly, a generous slug of sherry.

'Interesting,' Fergus said. 'If the garden designs don't take off you'd make a fascinating cook.'

Clancy said indignantly, 'My business *has* taken off. I'm on my way to becoming a name in a year or so. And I never wanted to do anything else.'

She held out hands that felt strange without the ring. 'Green fingers,' she said. 'I always had them.' Her eyes shone with happy memories. 'When my father was alive we had an old gardener. He taught me how to pick out plants, what would grow where, and let me do odd gardening jobs. I always knew I should enjoy that more than any other way of life. Although sometimes I dreamt of becoming a lawyer and joining my father's firm.'

'Why didn't you?'

Academically she could have qualified, but her sights had always been set on horticultural college, and she said frankly, 'Because the only reason was that I'd have been working with Hugh. His father and mine were the senior partners then. It was a pure pipe-dream. No other job would give me half the satisfaction I get designing my gardens.' Her enthusiasm seemed to be intriguing him. He was listening closely, and she asked him, 'Do you have a garden?'

'A townhouse with a patio.'

'I'm good with patios. I could design yours.'

'You haven't seen my patio.'

She laughed. 'Dress designers must look at folk and

imagine how they'd like to dress them. I plan gardens in my head for the people I meet. Maybe something featuring stainless steel for you.'

'What?'

'Or slate and well-weathered ironwork.'

'No flowers?'

'I haven't come to flowers yet. I don't seem to be getting past a lot of black foliage.'

'That sounds a riot.' She couldn't decide what setting she could picture him in. Maybe not a garden at all; wide open spaces, city streets, a war zone. She couldn't look at him and believe she knew what he wanted in a garden, in anything.

'I'd never offer you a rose garden.'

She'd been joking, but when he asked, 'What did you design for Hugh?' she wished he hadn't asked.

Her earliest dream garden had had Hugh walking with her down an avenue of tall trees towards a gazebo on a hill. He had always been her dream lover. 'If I ever did,' she said shortly, 'it was so long ago I've forgotten. How did you start? What made you go looking for trouble to write about?'

'I didn't,' he said. 'I was on holiday, on the slopes of an extinct volcano. Only it wasn't extinct. It blew, and I sold an eye-witness account to a press agency. Now I have contacts and contracts. I get sent and I go looking. Half the time I swear trouble waits for me.'

She nodded, agreeing. 'I'm sure you could pitch your tent and blow a volcano. If I did design your patio I'd make it flameproof.'

She laughed again, and their eyes met, and what she had just said must have made her imagine something like an electric spark between them. A blinding threatening flash that made her shrink back and quickly look away.

He got up from the table, gathering the soup bowls, carrying them to the sink; and from feeling lively enough to go on talking all night she was suddenly worn out. She couldn't hold back a yawn and she didn't try. She wriggled her shoulders, flexing the muscles that were stiff, and said, 'I'm tired. I'll have to call it a day.'

'See you in the morning,' he said. 'Come on, then.' That was to the dog, who bounced to the door while the man took off shoes and pulled on rubber boots, then picked up a torch.

'Are you taking him out?' That was so obvious he didn't answer. 'What's it like out there?'

When he opened the door she went to see for herself, peering into darkness. No moon, no stars. No light except from the ray of the torch. But the rain had stopped, and there seemed to be a wider path around the house so the water must be going down. 'Can I come?' she asked.

'I don't think so.'

'It wouldn't take a minute to put on a coat and change my shoes.'

'No.' He followed the dog outside and she wondered why she had wanted to go with him. She let the door close, because he would not have waited and hadn't she just said how tired she was? It had been a good day, and after another night's sleep she was pretty sure that tomorrow would be worth waking up for.

Even knowing what was waiting for her in less than three days' time couldn't stop her feeling that while she was here she would have no more nightmares about Hugh.

When she woke her first thought was of Hugh and Susan, then she smelled breakfast cooking and jumped out of bed. The view from the window was bleak, mudflats and a pewter-grey sky, but she padded along to the bathroom, showered and washed her hair, towelling it almost dry. Then she got into a pair of well-cut black pants, the sky-blue shirt and the cashmere sweater.

Hugh's photograph smiled up at her from her case again. She would have done better to have freaked out by smashing that rather than throwing the ring away. But the ring had gone and the photograph was still smiling. It was all such a mess that she should have been sick with worry. She couldn't believe she was feeling so cheerful.

'One egg or two?' Fergus said. He was at the stove and there were two glasses of what looked like fresh orange juice on the table.

'I'm not much for breakfast,' she began. She usually started her day on coffee and cereal, hurrying over that, but today she was a lady of leisure. She had no timetable, and no plans except to be fit and strong when she left here.

She said, 'One egg, please.'

'And ham,' he said. 'This place is famous for its ham and eggs.'

'Is it?'

'Have I ever lied to you?'

'Never,' she said. 'But I bet you play a mean game of poker.'

The ham and eggs were good. After breakfast

Fergus went to the desk in the visitors' lounge, while Clancy relaxed by the kitchen stove and read her books.

Mid-morning she brewed coffee and took in a cup for him while she replaced her Victorian novel, telling him, 'It did end in tears. I don't want another from that shelf.'

He pulled out a deep drawer in the desk that had boxed games, jigsaws, packs of cards, and she delved into that, took out a jigsaw and two card packs. 'This hotel should have three stars at least with all this exciting entertainment laid on,' she said.

She did the jigsaw—horses running wild—on a corner of the big kitchen table. She couldn't remember the last time she had frittered away a day like this, but she felt it was recharging her batteries better than a health farm. They ate toasted cheese sandwiches for lunch and made an evening meal of fluffy Spanish omelettes. And when the mobile phone rang she would have liked to switch it off before it shattered the fantasy that this was a secret island where no one could get at her.

Of course nobody was getting at her, the call was for Fergus, and she stood up to leave the room so that he could take it in private. But he waved her back to her chair and spoke for a few minutes to a caller who had to be enquiring how he was and where the floods had reached. No problems, he was saying, everything was in hand. When he put down the phone he asked Clancy, 'Any calls you want to make?'

Business calls could wait, and so could Hugh, although perhaps she should speak to her mother. Esta Lindhurst could be touchy if she was not getting all the attention she expected, and she might be expecting a call from her daughter by now. 'I'd better ring home and speak to my mother,' Clancy said.

Her mother's girlish voice answered and told her she had just missed Hugh, who had called in on his way from the courts. Clancy said she would be home the day after tomorrow, and then listened to a rambling account of her mother's search for a pair of shoes to match an outfit.

At last Clancy said, 'I must go. I'm glad you found the shoes.' She put down the phone and apologised. 'My mother does run on.'

'Everything's all right?'

'Yes, she's bought a pair of shoes and Hugh dropped in for a coffee.'

'Your mother gets on with Hugh?'

'More than that. She idolises him.' Her mother often said it had been the happiest day of her life when Hugh and Clancy decided to marry. If their engagement broke up it would break her mother's heart.

'What am I going to do?' Clancy sighed, looking at her ringless hand. 'I can't pretend nothing has happened.'

'Not unless you come up with a better excuse for ditching the heirloom,' said Fergus.

She hadn't opened the packs of cards she had brought in with the jigsaw. She had thought she might play patience with the ordinary pack; the other was a Tarot set. She had no idea how the Tarot worked, but there was a booklet of instructions and she pulled that out with the pack.

'Let's see if the cards have an answer,' she said, and, when one of his eyebrows shot up in quizzical surprise, 'Well, I haven't, and it doesn't sound as if you have.'

'Leave me out of this game,' he said.

It was a game. She was not superstitious. She sometimes read her horoscope, and sometimes her dreams seemed to have hidden meanings, but she was not opening the booklet and fanning the cards face down because she expected them to guide her in any way. She was playing a game.

A complicated one going by the instructions. 'The first step is to learn the meaning of each separate card,' she read aloud. 'So...' She turned up one of a falling tower and found it on the list. '"The struck tower—betrayal and ruin." That's a good start. They can only get better.'

She went on smiling as she turned up the next card, a grinning skeleton dragging a scythe, and read out, '"Death means death".'

There was nearly a whole pack to go. This was sheer chance, and didn't mean a thing, but a shiver ran down her spine like the trail of a thin cold finger and she forced a laugh that sounded false. 'I don't think I want to play this game.'

'It said learn what they mean; it didn't say take them personally,' Fergus reminded her, and she knew that, but she gathered up the cards and stacked them back into the box. 'Tell me about some of the gardens you've designed,' he said.

Soon she was relaxing again, talking and listening, telling him about a garden she was designing round an old water mill, laughing at tales he told her as the hours passed so lazy and comfortable that even the silences seemed soothing. She didn't feel she had to fill them with chatter, and although it was late and she was tired she was reluctant to call it a day.

Some time around midnight, with her head on a

cushion in a corner of the sofa, she dozed off, waking when he woke her. 'Time for bed.' She could hardly raise her heavy eyelids. She knew where she was, who she was with, but she was still dopey, because for a moment she thought that he was going to lift her off the sofa, into his arms, and carry her to their bed.

She sat up straighter and shook herself wide awake. 'Goodness, how long have I been asleep?'

'Five minutes, ten.'

Of course he didn't take her in his arms. He didn't even help her to her feet. And of course she hadn't wanted him to. He said, 'You need your rest.'

'I must do.' And this time she was the one who said, 'See you in the morning.'

In bed she didn't fall asleep at once. For a while her mind drifted back over what had been a really enjoyable day.

One more day and she would be leaving. It had stopped raining, but her van had been in the open through the worst of the downpours. The engine might not fire; the plugs could be waterlogged. That would be a blip that could delay her departure. Perhaps she should check on these things tomorrow.

It happened to be Fergus who brought up the suggestion after breakfast. 'Should we take a look at your van?'

Clancy almost found herself saying, It'll be all right. But she changed it to, 'I was thinking of that myself.'

The engine purred beautifully at the first touch of the ignition and all around the floods had receded into mud and puddles. There was nothing to stop her leaving any time, but there was no reason why she should until tomorrow, and she wanted this last day and night.

She said, 'I'm going for a walk. Will you come with me?'

'Sure,' he said. 'You'll be needing gumboots.'

There were several pairs in a cloakroom. She found a size that fitted and a lightweight waterproof and then walked with Fergus, and Bruno the dog, on the higher grounds around the hotel, where the turf squelched and gravel and paving stones gleamed wet. In spite of the limp he walked with the co-ordinated ease of a born athlete. Then they went down the slippery slope to the river and the little bridge.

The river was still flowing fast although it was shallower. She couldn't have touched the surface now, leaning over the low wall. As she looked down she felt Fergus's hand on her shoulder and said, 'You don't think—'

'I don't think you're jumping, but I don't want you losing your balance again. What are you looking for? The ring's long gone.'

'I know that. If it ever does get washed up I know it will be miles from here.' She bit her lip, recalling ruefully, 'It was a bit loose, and Hugh wanted it made a better fit, but I wouldn't take it off.'

She had been so sure that she would never be parted from her ring as long as she lived. 'In a million years nobody would expect me to throw it away,' she said. It had been the last thing she had expected herself.

Fergus burst out laughing. 'It was quite a gesture.'

He could laugh. While she was here the ring-dumping seemed so crazy that it was comic. When she got home it would be a very serious matter. But with Fergus here a little madness didn't go amiss, it was easy to laugh.

She felt the exhilaration of a teenager having fun, without a care in the world.

'Race you back,' she said, and took off up the steep muddy path, hampered by her gumboots, but on long strong legs which gave her an advantage over a man with only one good leg.

Behind her Fergus called, 'This is not a fair contest.'

'You can't stand competition, that's your problem,' she shouted back. 'Come on, Bruno, race you to the top.'

The dog was careering all over the place, splattering mud everywhere, and Clancy slithered as she climbed. It was wonderful, being healthy again. She reached the top of the path and whirled round in triumph, with Fergus a few paces behind and Bruno still tearing up and down. She was doing a victory jig when the dog hurtling at her knocked her flat.

She sank into the wet ground with a horrible sloshing sound, and when she sat up the mud tried to suck her down again. Fergus stood over her. 'What is it that pride goes before?' he said cheerfully.

'Oh, shut up. Did you teach him to do that?'

'Knock women down? Absolutely not.' He stooped to help her stand, still grinning.

'Thank you,' she said, and she reached up to cup his face in her hands, transferring most of the mud that caked her gloves onto his face and into his hair.

There could have been a rough and tumble. Like a snowball fight, only stickier and messier. She would have loved to slosh mud at him and have a mad tussle, screaming with laughter. Briefly she considered wrapping herself around him and rubbing off yet more mud, but thought better of it when he said, 'One more move and you won't get the bathroom first.'

'And I thought you were a gentleman.'

'Oh, no, you didn't.'

'No, I never did. And as for you,' she said to the dog, that was panting with lolling tongue as if it was grinning too, 'I don't know what you're laughing at, the state you're in, and *you're* certainly not getting into the bathroom before me.'

Just inside the kitchen door she leaned against the wall, balancing on one leg while she struggled with her gumboots. As they were coated with mud she couldn't get a real grip on them, and Fergus said, 'Let me,' tugging off first one then the other.

'Am I suppose to pull your boots off now?' she enquired.

'I've got to hosepipe him down first. You get cleaned up, then I'll let you know if there's anything you can do for me.' He leered like a melodrama villain.

'Dream on,' she chortled, and giggled her way to the bathroom.

The waterproof and boots had protected her clothes, but there was mud in her hair and she showered again. When she stepped out she was glowing. Not just from the fast climb and the shower but with an inner excitement that was making her skin tingle.

She got back into bra and briefs and into her dressing gown, a heavy cream satin. She would dress completely when her hair was dry. It was dripping now, and she wrapped a towel around her head.

In the kitchen the dog's coat was sleek and shining, and there were no signs of mud on Fergus. He was out of his gumboots and he had either used another bathroom or stuck his head under the tap at the kitchen sink.

Clancy sat down in front of the stove, took the towel off her head and shook her hair loose. The fire burned brightly between the bars, warming her face and her throat and the curve of her breasts where the robe fell open.

She smiled across at Fergus and he came and knelt beside her. She knew he would take the towel from her, and she closed her eyes and drifted into a blissful mini-trance, feeling his fingers through the thickness of the towel easing away every trace of tension. The lightest of touches went deep, so that she was all sensation, all feeling, floating in a warm sea under a hot sun.

Then he said, 'Do you think this is a good idea?'

That reached her. When she looked into his face she came right out of her trance. Her robe had slipped from her shoulders and she hitched it up. 'I was nearly asleep again. It must be the air round here.' She ran her fingers through her hair and began to babble. 'That's dry enough. I ought to be able to shove it into some sort of style now. Your hair dries itself, I suppose. You can't beat a good cut. Who's your stylist?'

He said, 'You are joking,' and she laughed, as if she were, but when she got into her bedroom she knew this was no joke.

She had been drifting into a willing seduction with no thought of resistance or even protest. How could she blame Hugh and Susan when she would have done the same thing herself? And it would have meant no more than—what had Fergus said? A temporary surge of hormones. A holiday affair. She had friends who took them for granted, although they had never appealed to Clancy. And since she'd been engaged to Hugh she had never looked at another man.

Not until the fates had washed her up into the arms of a man who could be sexual dynamite. She shouldn't be staying here for another night. She was fit enough to drive and another night here might be a terrible mistake. She must get away, go home right now.

She dressed and packed, then went into the kitchen and said, 'I should be on my way. I really can't afford to be taking this time off.'

He didn't sound surprised or concerned. He said it had been good meeting her, as you might say getting away from someone at a party without wanting to see them again.

They went in the van with her down the track through the trees to the main road. Then the man and the dog got out and Fergus said, 'Drive carefully.'

When she turned for a last look back they had gone, and she was missing him already. So badly that she almost stopped the van and ran after him. But that would have been insane. She put her foot down on the accelerator, her eyes in the driving mirror showing strain until she forced herself to look calmer. She drove steadily, gaining speed, getting away. 'You're on your own now, girl,' she said aloud. Which was stupid when she had so many friends, a doting mother, and the lover she had always loved.

By the time she turned her car into the drive of the house she shared with her mother she was still undecided how she would handle the matter of Susan, but confident that it could be done. She couldn't give Hugh up over what, as Fergus had said, might have been a one-off lapse. She would be cool and in control and everything would work out, because Hugh loved her as much as she loved him.

Her mother, dressed in a slick Chanel-type suit, her

ash-blonde hair simply but expensively styled, came
into the hall as Clancy opened the front door. Esta
Lindhurst took very good care of herself and Clancy
had always been proud of her pretty, fashionable
mother.

She smiled happily, seeing Clancy. 'I didn't expect
you till tomorrow.'

'Well, here I am,' said Clancy, and her mother's
smile became coy.

'You wanted to get back to Hugh. Does he know
you're here?'

'No.'

'You must phone him.'

Clancy was not getting in touch with Hugh until
she'd decided what she was going to say to him, but
her mother was already picking up the receiver.
Clancy took the phone from her, replaced it and said,
'I've got unpacking to do, and there's some business
to attend to. I'm not looking my best just now. I'll get
organised and contact him in the morning. He's not
expecting me till then.'

'You mean, not tell him you're home?'

Esta could not understand this, and when Clancy
said, 'That is what I mean,' the shadow of a frown
creased her mother's smooth forehead.

'Is everything all right?' she asked anxiously.

'Of course,' Clancy said.

She brought her cases in from the car and took them
up to her bedroom. This had been Clancy's room since
it had been prepared for her as a nursery before she
was born, although lately she had shared Hugh's bedroom often enough for her toothbrush to be in his bathroom, with some of her make-up on his dressing table
and some of her clothes in his wardrobe. She might

never be able to lie on that bed again without thinking of Susan in Hugh's arms, or look into the big gold-framed mirror without seeing the images of Hugh and Susan like an erotic painting.

She sat down on her own single bed, letting herself sink so that her cheek was on a pillow. If she crashed out for a few minutes she might wake with a clearer head. Right now she was confused, and there was nobody here she could confide in.

Her mother would take Hugh's side; she would find some excuse for him. Most of Clancy's friends might blame Susan, who had a name for looking on men as fair game, but some of them had been ex-girlfriends of Hugh themselves. And Clancy, who had always been a private person beneath her high spirits and zest for living, shrank from the idea of her heartache becoming general gossip.

She heard the hall door close. Her mother was probably on her way out. After that she must have slept, because the ringing doorbell woke her. It was late enough to need a light to be switched on as the caller pressed the bell a second time and kept it ringing. No one answered so Clancy came downstairs.

Hugh stood on the doorstep, and her heart missed a beat. Before she could speak he said, 'Hello, darling,' and he was in the hall with her, closing the door behind him.

'What's all this about not telling me you were home?' he said. Her mother, of course. Now he was holding her close. She could smell the very expensive aftershave that she always bought him, and he was smiling boyishly at her. Hugh was years older than Clancy but he could have passed for her age. 'I'll forgive you,' he said teasingly, 'if you don't go away again. There wasn't a minute, night or day, when I wasn't missing you.'

She heard herself say, 'How about in bed?' And before he could follow what he thought was a cue for sexy talk she said flatly, 'I came back. I saw you with Susan.'

He flinched as though from a blow, the healthy ruddiness of his face turning pasty. For a few seconds, as his lips tightened, his features seemed to sharpen and age. Then he groaned, 'Oh, God,' his hands falling from her to cover his face. 'I'm sorry, I'm sorry, I'm so sorry.'

She had not meant to blurt it out like that. What should she do now everything was out in the open? She couldn't lose him, but she couldn't say, Forget it; it doesn't matter, because it mattered horribly. When she said nothing he said humbly, 'I love you with all my heart, and only you.'

They had been the most wonderful words she had ever heard when he'd first said them. After an Easter ball when he was driving her home. 'I love you, Clancy, will you marry me?' It had seemed then that all her dreams were coming true, because Hugh loved her; she was the one he wanted.

Now he was telling her, 'What happened with Susan will never happen again. It meant nothing.'

She bit harder on her lip as he went on, 'I'm dealing with her lease; you know that. The papers were in my study at home and she came over to discuss them. Your phone rang in the bedroom and I went up to answer it.' His trained lawyer's voice was getting into the swing of the story now. 'It was a business call for you; I made a note. Susan came in and she was—well, you know Susan.'

Clancy had seen the red dress on the pale beige carpet as she'd gone up the stairs. Briefly and horrifically it had looked like blood, and then she had seen it was a dress, and in the mirror through the open doorway she had seen the bed.

She could imagine Susan continuing the striptease as she sashayed into the bedroom, and Hugh taking what was on offer. She said ironically, 'So it was all Susan's fault? You just couldn't help yourself?' And he was crestfallen again.

'Of course it wasn't. It was my fault. I was criminally irresponsible and I'd do anything in the world not to have hurt you. If you hadn't come back you wouldn't have been hurt. Please, Clancy, believe me. Never again I promise you. Never, ever again.'

He reached for her and she took a stumbling step away. It couldn't be settled like this. 'I need some time to think,' she said.

She was not being rushed into pretending nothing much had happened. After that first shock Hugh would be sure he could coax her round, and she must be resenting his conceit, because she said, 'It's a funny old world. While I was away I met someone else.'

His lips tightened again, but almost at once he smiled.

'Don't you believe me?' she said.

His voice was tender. 'I believe that any man would flirt with you, given half the chance, and you have every right to be angry with me. I was a selfish swine. But you know that Susan means nothing. I'll always love you. We were meant to be together.'

She said, 'Not tonight, we're not. Not for a good many nights.' She opened the front door and stood

well to one side, discouraging any idea he might have
of trying an embrace as he passed her.

'I'm so sorry,' he said again. Tomorrow he would
beg for her forgiveness again, and each time her resistance would probably weaken, but she couldn't give
in this easily.

She listened to his car drive away and sat on the
bottom of the stairs, dreading her mother coming
home. Her mother would expect to find Hugh here,
the pair of them all lovey-dovey. When he wasn't she
would want to know why, and she was soon going to
find out there was friction. Then there would be never-
ending arguments and accusations.

Clancy longed for the magic of the little hotel, cut
off from the world. The one person she could talk to
about this was Fergus. She had the number of his mobile. She had left one of her cards, with home and
office phone numbers, on the dresser in the kitchen,
so some time he might phone her. But tonight she
couldn't wait for a call that might not come. She
needed to talk to him now. She sat on her bed, her
feet tucked beneath her, and punched out his number.

When he answered she nearly joked nervously, This
is Angela. But as soon as she'd said hello he said,
'What's happening?'

'You know who it is?'

'Of course I do. I was going to phone you. Is everything all right? How did you explain the ring?'

She gave a little screech. 'Nobody knows about the
ring yet. That's another crisis for tomorrow. Are you
sitting comfortably?'

'I'm listening.'

'I was going to be cool about this. I wasn't going
to do anything until tomorrow. But Hugh found out I

was back and he came round and I sort of lost my head.'

'You haven't shot him?'

'That isn't funny.'

'You can be a violent lady.'

'Nobody hit anybody. He was sorry it happened and terribly sorry I saw them. If I hadn't seen them it wouldn't have changed anything because—like you said—it meant nothing. And he swears it won't happen again.'

'A natural pleader,' Fergus drawled. 'A born lawyer.'

'What should I do?'

'You seem to be managing.'

'I'm not. He is.' She was jabbering into the mouthpiece. 'I don't want Hugh crowding me too soon. I'd like to hold him off for a while.' Her laughter was hollow. 'I even told him I'd met someone else while I was away.'

'And?' Fergus prompted.

'He wasn't bothered about that. He's very sure of me.'

'He sounds a charmer.'

'Oh, he is.' And she sounded such a drip.

'What you need,' said Fergus, 'is someone to keep you out of the arms of the law until you're sure that's where you want to be. And who better than the mystery man you met while you were away?'

'What?'

'There's an old Chinese proverb that says if you've saved someone's life that gives you a responsibility in their future. You're more or less bound to keep an eye out for them as a sort of perpetual minder.'

This time her laughter was genuine. 'I've never heard that one. It seems tough on the rescuer.'

'Tough birds, the old Chinese,' said Fergus. 'See you soon.' And he rang off before she could say, Don't come here.

She should be calling him back and saying no...but she had used the first excuse she'd had to phone him and talk to him.

If he did come the already explosive situation could blow like a volcano. He would certainly send her mother—and Hugh—ballistic. But she sat on the bed, hugging her knees to her chest, experiencing a warm glow in her stomach at the thought of seeing him again.

CHAPTER FOUR

CLANCY left the house next morning before her mother was awake. Last night Esta had looked into Clancy's bedroom and Clancy had deliberately pretended to be deep asleep. It might be cowardly to let things ride until Fergus was here but it could do no harm, and Clancy had plenty of work to busy herself.

The walled garden of her home had not changed since her childhood. The trees and lawns and flowerbeds were in the same design. This was Esta's garden, and she did not want her daughter playing around with it, but through a gate in the wall was a field that had been three acres of old trees, rough grasses and brambles. Over years of planning and back-breaking slog that had become Clancy's garden, where a garden house was her office studio.

It had rained here too while she had been away. Nothing like the deluge of flash floods, but everywhere seemed to have been washed clean and the air smelled fresh and cold.

Elizabeth, generally known as Bets, halfway through a six-month work experience and with every intention of staying because she liked the job and she liked working with Clancy, was already at her desk. She was a bright-eyed eighteen-year-old, with ginger hair that frizzed no matter what she did to it and freckles she hated, although her boyfriend kept telling her they were cute.

She was glad to see Clancy. The place was livelier

with Clancy around, and it had been a responsibility on her own. She said, 'You're back early. How was it?'

Clancy got out of her coat and hung it in a cupboard. 'The exhibition? I didn't get there. I changed my mind.'

Clancy had all sorts of suppliers; she would have been on business somewhere, Bets knew. She said, 'It was a break for you anyway.'

'Sure was,' said Clancy. 'Anything exciting happened here?'

Bets giggled. 'No such luck.' She enjoyed a bit of excitement.

There were matters to deal with. Plans Clancy had produced for an awkwardly shaped garden and equally awkward clients seemed to be finally getting their approval. There was an enquiry from someone who had just moved into a brand-new house on a building site and wanted a mature cottage garden by the spring. A couple of phone calls came through, one from a firm producing equipment for children's gardens, the other trying to sell Clancy advertising space in a country magazine. Then there was a call from Hugh.

Bets answered that one. Clancy was starting on a lay-out, measuring and drawing the boundary freehand on the tracing paper, and when Bets said, 'Yes, she's right here,' she knew from Bets's happy grin who it was.

She reluctantly put down her pencil and took up the phone, and said, 'Hugh? Look, I'm very busy. I can't talk now.'

'This won't take a minute. I've booked a table for two at the Gateway for tonight.'

That was one of their favourite restaurants, but wild

horses wouldn't drag Clancy there yet. Any one of their special dishes would choke her.

She said crisply, 'Sorry, I can't. I've other plans.'

She clicked down the phone and Bets's mouth fell open. Bets was no fool. That was Hugh Clancy had just snapped at, and Clancy was not wearing her ring.

Now she was putting her overcoat on again, buttoning it up with quick impatient fingers as if she couldn't wait to get out of here. 'I'll be at the water mill,' she said, and she was gone, with a swirl of her dark red hair, before Bets could find the courage to wail, 'You *haven't* had a row?'

Hugh would very likely be ringing Clancy's mother, and if he caught Esta she would be after Clancy. Not yet, Clancy thought. I need reinforcements before I face the pair of you. I need Fergus, who is not taking any of this seriously but will stop me being yanked back by Hugh until I am good and ready.

The old water mill stood where a river had been diverted into a millpond in a village about six miles out of town, and for nearly four years now it had been somewhere that never failed Clancy. When she was over-stressed even a few minutes alone there could calm her down, and on the rare occasion when she needed a shot of adrenaline she could walk round the mill house and grounds and flashes of inspiration would come into her mind. She was going to do fantastic things here.

Her mother said it gave her the creeps, Hugh said it could give anyone rheumatism, but Clancy loved it, and she was sure they both would when she had spent much more money and done much more work on it.

Today she parked her van in the village street and walked down the narrow lane that had been a cobbled road when horse-drawn wagons brought wheat to be ground into flour. In the mill house she sat at a window for a while, with a sketchpad, making notes for a rock garden in weathered local stone. And then she walked around outside, reaching the bridge near the great wheel, looking down into the water. It was nothing like the last river she had watched, that had been a torrent, although the coincidence was reinforced when a big black dog came bounding along.

Behind Bruno strode Fergus. 'What is it with you and bridges over troubled waters?' he asked when he reached her.

She had been waiting for him to come today, but happiness bubbled in her. She was laughing, stroking Bruno's head, hugging Fergus, letting go quickly but still grinning from ear to ear, asking him, 'Who's minding the hotel?'

'The couple who usually do.'

'How did you get here? How did you know I was here?'

He held her loosely, capable hands cupping her elbows, smiling down at her, telling her, 'The car's automatic; it's an easy drive. I rang your office and got a very obliging girl who told me where you were and gave me instructions how to get here.'

'It's our Bets,' said Clancy. 'She is helpful. Thanks for coming. I'm glad to see you.'

She thought he hesitated. If he did it was only for a moment before he turned so that his arm was light around her shoulders. On the bridge the wind was cold and damp. 'Shall we go into the house?' she said. 'I could brew coffee.'

'Sounds good.'

Inside the house the rough walls were colour-washed while downstairs was a kitchen-living room and a small bathroom above two unused rooms. The living room was sparsely furnished but there was a Calor gas heater and stove and Clancy filled a kettle at a stone sink and put it on one of the stove's rings to boil.

Bruno flopped down on a dark red Turkish rug Clancy had bought on last year's holiday and Fergus sat on a three-seater divan and watched her until she joined him. She said, 'Hugh told me he went upstairs to answer the phone—my mobile I'd left behind. This was in his house; they'd been in his office. The phone was in the bedroom and Susan followed him in.'

'She would, wouldn't she? Him being such a charmer.'

There was nothing to laugh at, nothing had hurt her like this, but the lift of a corner of his mouth showed what Fergus thought, and she heard herself saying, 'It gets crazier, like something out of a French farce. It seems Susan was doing a striptease when Hugh looked up from the phone.'

'He told you this?'

'She'd taken off her dress on the way upstairs. I saw it, a red silk dress, and, knowing Susan, I should think her undies were red silk too.'

Fergus said, 'Well, I haven't met either of them, but I get the picture. It must have been—er—colourful.'

Suddenly Clancy was imagining Susan, skipping around, shedding bra, whatever, like Salome of the seven veils. And she started to laugh until somehow tears were fighting the laughter and her face was pressed into Fergus's shoulder, muffling her sobs and hiccups while she fought to control both. When she raised her face she rubbed damp cheeks with the back of her hand and said unsteadily, 'Sorry about that. I've left a damp patch on your jacket.'

'Considering you've had me soaked to the skin more than once, what's a damp patch?' he said.

With anyone else she would have been embarrassed, shrieking with laughter and sobbing at the same time like somebody demented. But with Fergus she could dig in her pocket for a tissue, wipe her eyes, and she was almost all right again.

'How long can you stay?' she asked.

'As long as it takes,' he said.

Until his leg had healed? Until he'd finished whatever work he was doing during his convalescence? Or until her problem with Hugh was settled?

She would have enquired, but he said, 'Can you recommend a local hotel?'

An old school-friend of Clancy's ran a lovely old inn in the High Street, but she found herself suggesting, 'You could stay here.'

'In this house? Who owns it?'

'It's mine.' She always got a glow of pride over that, and she smiled, like a pussycat, almost purring. 'I bought it with a trust fund my father set up for me at twenty-one. It was falling into a ruin, and I spent all my money on it, but it's going to be a real show-place some time.'

'It's pretty good now.'

'I've furnished it with what I've picked up in junk shops and boot sales, but it's liveable-in. Friends stay here sometimes. You're welcome, if you like.'

'I'd like that very much.'

She showed him how the stove worked, how the sofa unfolded into a bed, and promised, 'I'll get some bedding from home. All right,' she said, and before he could do any testing of springs she had pushed the bed back into a sofa.

If he'd lain down he might possibly have drawn her down too. Sobbing against his shoulder had been consoling, but lying full length against him might trigger a dangerous reaction. She remembered how she had melted under his touch when he was drying her hair. That wasn't surprising. He was a seriously attractive man.

They could have been passionate friends, but she was a one-man woman and all she wanted from Fergus was friendship, so she must be careful not to take any risks that might put another spin on the relationship.

She said, 'Sorry the coffee's instant. I keep a jar and some biscuits here, but that's all there is in the cupboard. I'll show you the nearest shop for some food. And for him.'

Bruno ate custard cream biscuits with them while they drank instant coffee, and Clancy told Fergus about some of her friends he would be meeting if he was staying.

'Do many of them go in for striptease?' he asked, as if it was a serious question.

'I'll point Susan out to you,' she said solemnly. 'She's the expert.'

She was quite looking forward to showing him off, although there were going to be ructions with her mother and Hugh. In the end Fergus would leave and life would go on, with Clancy and Hugh together again. But the next few weeks could be exciting, and they might make Hugh take her less for granted in future.

It was late afternoon, getting dark, when she said,

'I'll show you the shop and then, if you like, I'll show you my home.'

His car, an automatic Range Rover, was parked behind hers in the village street. They walked, with Bruno between them, to a row of half a dozen small shops, only a few minutes away, tethered the dog to railings and went in to buy basic foodstuffs, including large tins and packs of dog biscuits. With this dumped in the mill house they set off again, this time in the two cars, Fergus following Clancy.

Hugh's car was in the driveway of her home. She should have expected he might be here, and she wondered what he was telling her mother. Not the whole truth, she'd bet.

It was a wide drive. Clancy edged her car round Hugh's and into the garage. Fergus drew up alongside, got out and waited for her.

'It's Hugh's car,' she said. 'Would you like to meet him?'

'Damn right I would,' he said, and she had her first misgiving over whether she should be letting someone so forceful interfere in an affair of the heart that probably needed handling gently.

Nobody came into the hall when Clancy opened the front door with her key. She dropped her overcoat on a chair. Hugh and her mother had heard her coming, because Hugh was getting to his feet while Esta sat in her usual Georgian rosewood armchair, both of them smiling. So nothing unpleasant had happened yet. For a few seconds it was a scene that Clancy had often come home to. If she worked late and Hugh got away early he would come here and be waiting for her.

When they saw she was not alone her mother went on smiling. Esta's social smile was flirtatious for attractive young men, and this one certainly caught her eye.

Clancy introduced them. 'My mother and Hugh Marshall. This is Fergus McKenzie.'

She had not described Hugh as her fiancé. That might have been why Hugh was straightening up, very much the successful professional. He was good at that. In spite of his boyish looks he had a confidence that impressed most folk, both in court and out of it. He was always expensively dressed, handsome as an up-and-coming actor, and Clancy was used to his charm putting every other man in the shade.

But not this time. Fergus was taller, thinner, with a harder face and an air of something that could be menace. His smile was tight lipped, his eyes were hooded, and she thought Hugh swallowed before he asked, 'Have we met before?'

Fergus said, 'No, we have not,' his voice flat and quiet, and Clancy was scared he might be about to declare himself Hugh's rival here and now, just for the hell of it.

She stepped into the middle of the room to claim everyone's attention and said, 'Fergus and I met this week, while I was away.'

That registered with Hugh. A faint flush was starting just above his collar while Esta said chattily, 'You met at the exhibition? Are you a gardener?'

'I'm a journalist,' Fergus said, and Hugh tried a heartiness that didn't quite come off.

'Then what are you doing here?' he asked. 'Nothing particularly newsworthy going on in this town that I'm aware of.'

Fergus said, 'As a lawyer you must have a few cases that make the headlines.'

Hugh headed a prosperous legal firm, but their business was rarely sensational, and as this character knew Hugh was a lawyer Clancy must have discussed him with McKenzie. Hugh wondered what else she had said and resisted an impulse to glare.

Clancy said, 'Fergus was staying at the hotel, working on a book. I've offered him the mill house for a few days.'

Esta saw nothing in that; Clancy's friends did sometimes move into the old mill, although it was not a place where Esta would have cared to stay the night. But Hugh had a different opinion. The flush crept high up his neck and he asked, 'Why? It must have been a very sleazy hotel not to be better than the old mill.'

'He thinks he'll be able to work there,' said Clancy, 'and it seemed the least I could do after he saved my life.'

Her mother and Hugh gasped, then stared, then almost together they said, *'What?'*

Fergus, she thought, looked as if he might be auditioning her, waiting to hear her go on with her piece. She said, 'I was caught in the floods—you must have seen them on TV or read about them. Well, I got out of my van on a bridge and I got swept into the river. I could have drowned, only Fergus pulled me out.'

Hugh gave a strangled groan. Her mother clutched her throat and croaked, 'But you're a good swimmer.'

'Not the way I was dressed,' said Clancy, and the memory of being weighed down with the swirling waters closing over her made her shiver, until her mother's little scream brought her sharply back to the present.

Esta was shaking like a leaf, and Clancy wished she had made her story less dramatic. She put her arms

round her mother, reassuring her, 'It did me no harm.
Except for catching a chill. And that's why I didn't
bother with the exhibition. I stayed in the hotel instead.
Fergus was convalescing from a leg injury. We were
two crocks together so we cheered each other up.'

'That was nice,' said Esta. Clancy had always made
friends easily, and her mother had no qualms about
another friend being this young man because Clancy
was going to marry Hugh, the nicest of them all and
the only man for Clancy.

Hugh was not cheered by what he was hearing. He
tried to put a proprietary hand on Clancy's shoulder
and felt her flinch away from him. 'We're very grateful to you,' he said to Fergus.

Esta, who had taken hold of Clancy's hand, yelped,
'Where's the ring?'

Clancy said, 'I lost it in the water.'

That nearly set her mother off again. Esta had been
as proud of that ring as Clancy had, and she began
wailing about how often Clancy had been warned she
should let Hugh have it made smaller. Wasn't it only
last month she had been twirling it round on her finger
and her mother had said, 'You're going to lose that
one day.' Well, now she had.

Esta's tears were about to flow at this second shock,
until Hugh said, 'It doesn't matter. All that matters is
that she's safe.'

Clancy felt tears prickle her own eyes. That was
generous and loving, because it had been a fabulous
ring, and if Fergus had not been there those words
might have been almost enough to make her forget
Susan.

She did smile weakly at Hugh, and he smiled at her.
Then he said to Fergus, in a voice charged with emo-

tion, 'We're deeply in your debt. I don't know how I'll ever repay you.'

'Don't even try,' said Fergus, and his voice had no emotion at all.

Clancy's mobile was on a side-table. Hugh saw her glance towards it and cleared his throat to say, 'I brought it round.'

All of them but Esta were visualising Hugh answering that phone by the bedside and Susan coming into the room.

Hugh said, 'I'd better be going.' He looked at Clancy. 'Hadn't I?'

She said, 'I'm needing an early night. I'll see you out.'

He bent to kiss Esta's cheek, and she patted his cheek and said, 'Thank you for the truffles.'

'My pleasure,' he said.

He closed the drawing room door behind himself and Clancy. In the hall he asked her, 'What did you tell him about us?'

Everything there was to tell. But she wasn't going into that. She said, 'That we'd been close but I was no longer sure how close.'

'Does he think he's in with a chance?'

'I don't know what he thinks; he's a deep one.' When it came to it she didn't know that much about Fergus herself. 'You wouldn't be jealous, would you?'

'Am I meant to be? Is that why you invited him here?' He had invited himself, but Hugh sounded as if this was *her* childish tactic. Hugh's smile was teasing and tolerant, 'That wouldn't work, my darling, and we both know why. You're angry with me, with every reason. But I love you and you love me, and there's no way that we won't be together for ever.'

Close to Hugh again, she could believe that.

'Of course you're grateful,' said Hugh. 'As we all are. But anything else you're feeling for him is infatuation. I'm sure of that. As sure as I am that this is the real thing.'

His arms were around her, holding her against the smooth cloth of his well-cut jacket and with that intoxicating aftershave making her head swim. It would have been lovely to raise her face for his kiss, but she stayed rigid, and that was when the drawing room door opened and Fergus came into the hall.

Hugh swore as Clancy jerked out of his arms. She didn't want Fergus thinking Hugh was making a puppet on a string of her. Her impulse was to say something snappish, only she couldn't think what, and Fergus said, 'Just checking on Bruno.'

'Who's Bruno?' Hugh asked.

'A very big dog,' said Clancy.

Fergus said, 'Like to meet him?'

'No, thank you,' said Hugh, and Clancy thought that was as well. If he got his vibes from his master, Bruno would not take to Hugh.

She went outside with the two men to their two cars. As he opened his door Hugh asked her, 'I'll see you tomorrow night?'

Friday nights when they had nothing else planned they had a standing date: meeting friends at a country club. There were always some there they had known for years and they always had a pleasant evening.

But tonight she said, 'Don't call for me. I may see you there.'

'I'll be waiting.' He raised her ringless hands to his lips. 'Goodnight, my darling,' he said huskily.

'Get in the car,' she said, as Bruno galloped towards

them. Through the car window Hugh was mouthing something and Fergus strolled over.

'Goodnight to you too,' said Fergus.

Hugh drove off fast and Fergus said, 'There goes a frustrated man.' There was moonlight tonight, scudding clouds, but enough light for her to see that Fergus was grinning. Fergus did not like Hugh. What she had told him had not made Hugh sound likeable, but Hugh had so many good qualities. She said defensively, 'He was very good about the ring.'

'Sure to be well insured,' Fergus said cynically.

Bruno was sniffing his way down the drive heading for the road when Fergus called him back and Clancy said, 'If he needs a run, how about a walk through the woods?'

'Through the woods?' On a darkish chilly night it sounded an odd suggestion, but she smiled.

'A very little wood, at the back of the house. My secret garden.'

'We'd like to see that.'

She explained as they went, 'My father's father built the house. It was heathland up here then and the field came with it. We played in there when I was a child and—have you ever read *The Secret Garden*?'

'Not that I can remember.'

'I don't suppose you have. Well, that was the one Victorian book with a happy ending. The orphan girl who comes to an old house where there's a secret garden, and when she brings that back to life everything changes for the better. When I read the book I began to think what I could do with the field, and my father said go ahead, it was my field. But I didn't start serious planning until I was through college. Five years ago that was.'

They were at the high wooden gate in the red brick wall. She had her hand on the latch when he said, 'You do a lot of dreaming,' and that stung because she had always been painstakingly practical. 'Dream gardens,' he drawled. 'Dream lovers.'

She should have known better than to babble nonsense to him. Well, he'd think it was nonsense. She gave a half-shrug. 'Better have dreams than nightmares.'

Her worst nightmare ever had been that first night at the little hotel. But she wasn't thinking about that when she spoke, and she doubted if he was thinking about it either, because he must have so many nightmarish memories of his own. Her gardens, her life among civilised folk were on another planet from the life he led.

It was too dark to see his eyes, but he was smiling. 'So are you going to show me the garden?' he said. And she opened the gate, looking up at the moon, waiting for a cloud to pass because by moonlight her little woodland had a fairytale atmosphere.

She had planned the three-acre field to seem much bigger than it was, with meandering paths of bark between the trees and light and shade filtering through the foliage of silver birch and mountain ash. Over a pebbled path sawn-off stepping stones from a tree trunk led to a moss-carpeted glade with a bench under a weeping willow while an old chestnut tree spread its boughs over another secret nook.

Bruno went purposefully down every path, getting lost and doubling back, occasionally barking at whatever was rustling in the undergrowth, while Clancy gave names to plants and bushes—hazelnut, guelder rose—telling Fergus where there would be bluebells in the spring.

Moonlight came and went so that sometimes she could see the tall man walking beside her clearly; other times he was almost in darkness. But she was glad she had brought him here. She wanted to show him the garden she had created from a meadow and his praise was gratifying.

When he told her he thought she had done wonders she was delighted. 'I told you I was a gardener,' she said gaily.

'I never doubted it.' He took her hand. 'Green fingers.'

Her fingers were pale in the shadows and she moved away to point out the timber-built garden house. 'I work from there,' she said. 'Call in any time, but I must be getting back now.'

It was chance, of course, that they hadn't touched each other before. Neither had stumbled and there had always been a little space between them, but suddenly it seemed to her that even hand-holding could be too close, and she went on brightly, 'If my mother knew I was wandering around here with you, not with Hugh, she'd be out with a torch looking for us.'

'Does he always bring chocolates?' asked Fergus wryly.

'Often. But not as often as he brings things for me. He is very generous.'

'When it suits him,' said Fergus.

'How can you say that?' she snapped. 'You don't know that. You don't like him, do you?'

'He's not exactly my type.'

'Well, almost everybody does like him. All the women round here have always gone for Hugh.'

'All of them?' Fergus gave a hoot of derision. 'Come off it.'

'Well, a lot of them do.' He knew how she was. She didn't need to admit it. 'Like me. We could just have been about to make up when you walked in on us.'

'I thought you might be.' Well, she had let him stop her giving in too soon. And he reminded her, 'I'm your minder. And in your own interests my advice is, play it cool.'

By now they had reached the gate in the wall and were stepping into her mother's territory. She said, 'I'm trying to, only it isn't all that easy.'

'I'll stay close enough to step between you if the need arises,' he said, and she imagined him moving in to hold Hugh away from her. Though loaded with charm, Hugh had none of Fergus's steel. This was a game to Fergus, but Clancy would have to lay down the rules.

She said, 'You're going to a lot of trouble.'

'I'm enjoying myself,' he said cheerfully. 'Your account of how we met was good. You could do no less than offer to put me up for a few days after I'd saved your life.'

It hadn't been a lie. She said, 'You did pull me out—after you pushed me in.'

'"Push" was never the word. And I liked the touch of losing your ring in the river.'

'So I did.'

'When he claims on insurance shall you tell him it was no accident?'

'None of your business.'

'True.'

They walked back to his car. He let the dog in first.

It sat on the back seat, paws drooped over the passenger seat, great head turning to make sure the man was following. 'What time do you get up in the morning?' Fergus asked.

'Around half-seven.'

'I'll ring you and you can brief me on your day.'

She didn't need this much supervision. She said, 'I'm not sure what I'll be doing after work.'

'We'll think of something.' When he caught her fingers again, kissed them and said, 'Goodnight, my own darling,' she was as startled as if he had kissed her mouth and laid hands on her breasts. Then she recognised a wicked mimicry of Hugh's goodnight and burst out laughing.

'Sleep well, light of my life,' she said, fluttering eyelashes like mad.

She was wearing a thick sweater and a medium-weight suit, but as the car went the chill of the night reached her. They had forgotten the bedding, and there were no blankets in the mill house. Serve him right, she thought, with an inward grin, for being so sarcastic about Hugh. And almost guiltily, as though the thought was disloyal, she wondered how much the ring was insured for.

CHAPTER FIVE

WHEN Clancy had unpacked last night she had left Hugh's photograph in her case instead of replacing it on her bedside table, where it usually stood when she was at home. For a while she would manage without, because, looking at that with drowsy eyes, she might reach for her phone to call him. She would miss him all through the night. She might toss for hours before she was relaxed enough to sleep. She sighed and pummelled the pillow, preparing for a restless night.

Until her ringing phone woke her. She must have slept heavily almost at once, and she picked up the phone, bringing it down to where she was lying, still only half awake. 'Hugh?' she mumbled. She must have been dreaming of him.

'Well, that means he isn't with you,' said Fergus.

That woke her up. Her little travelling clock said just before seven and she howled, 'I said half-seven.'

'Don't be such a stickler for details. Come and have breakfast with me.'

He sounded showered and shaved, full of beans and too healthy by half for a woman who had not yet crawled out of bed. She said, 'Some of us are workers. I've had my few days off; I don't have time for breakfasts with strange men.'

'Pity. I was getting used to your face in the mornings.' A few mornings were all, but she would remember them, and she would have liked to drive over to the mill house now, only that was out of the question.

'So where is golden boy expecting to see you tonight?' Fergus enquired.

She slid her feet into mules and her arms into a bathrobe, telling him between yawns, 'We belong to a country club and that's where we'll be tonight. *If* I go.'

'That's up to you.'

'Would you come with me?' Hugh had said he would be there, and Susan might well be around, but nobody would feel sorry for Clancy if Fergus were with her.

He said, 'I'll collect you.'

'Eight o'clock, then, and *please* don't make it seven.'

She was in before Bets this morning, at the drawing board when Bets arrived. 'Did he find you at the mill?' was Bets's greeting. 'He rang not long after you'd gone.' She giggled. 'I didn't get his name but he's got a very sexy voice.'

She was waiting expectantly. 'He found me,' said Clancy.

Something in her voice made Bets ask anxiously, 'That was all right, wasn't it, telling him where you were?'

Clancy nodded. 'Sure, he's a friend.' She added nonchalantly, 'I hadn't noticed, but I suppose he does have a sexy voice.'

It felt strange, after work, not to be getting ready for Hugh. Going to the club, they often took sports gear. It was a leisure centre, with swimming, and tennis courts, a gym. But on Friday nights there was dancing, as well as wining and dining, and tonight Clancy was avoiding any exertion that would leave her with damp hair and hastily applied make-up.

Whenever she'd had a spare moment during the day she had gone over her wardrobe in her mind, so that she had chosen what she was wearing before she got home and could spend all the time until eight o'clock pampering herself from head to foot and psyching herself up until she felt like a cover-girl.

She was in a white satin trouser suit and a brushed black mohair wrap that was warm as a coat. A dramatic combination with the red lights glinting in her dark hair, and strappy black velvet sandals with very high heels giving her extra height.

She waited for the car to arrive, watching from her bedroom window so that she could get out of the house before her mother decided to come to the door and say hello to Hugh. Esta was taking it for granted that Clancy was off with Hugh this Friday evening and she could go on thinking that for now.

So as soon as Clancy saw Fergus's car turn in from the road she grabbed her purse and ran downstairs. She was standing in the driveway as he drew up beside her. He leaned across to open the passenger door and ask, 'What's the hurry?'

She slid inside, her wrap tucked around her. 'My mother thinks I'll be with Hugh and I don't want to start going into that. Meeting Hugh and whoever else is at the club will be hassle enough.'

'You want to go?' He stopped the car at the end of the drive and turned to look at her.

She said, 'Turn right and keep straight on. Yes, I want to go; I've got to face them.' The car moved into the road with Fergus scanning the way ahead, his profile clean and hard against the shifting lights through the window. He looked tough and handsome and she was lucky to have him with her. Under his cool quiz-zical gaze she was less likely to create a scene, even if she came face to face with a smirking Susan.

She asked, 'Where's Bruno?'

'Guarding the mill.'

'Not that I mind having him with us, but I'm not really dressed for Bruno.'

He said, 'You look fantastic,' and although she had worked on it she was so ridiculously pleased that she felt herself blushing.

She gave directions—the club was on the outskirts of town—and for a few minutes they drove in silence. Then she asked, 'What does Angela look like?'

'Why?'

Because she was intrigued about a woman who thought she had claims on Fergus.

'You've met my mother,' she said, 'and the man I'm going to marry. You're on your way to meet sev-eral of my friends, probably including sexy Susan. But I don't know anything about anybody who's anything to do with you.'

He said abruptly, 'My parents died in a car crash when I was eighteen,' and that made her wince like a blow. She had lost her own father with no time to say goodbye.

'I'm so sorry,' she whispered.

'So was I; they were all the family I had.' She still had her mother, and Hugh had been her big brother even before she'd realised how she loved him. 'But,' said Fergus, in a voice that closed that chapter of his life, 'I have some good friends you can meet whenever you like. Women, yes. No one in particular and certainly not Angela, who looks like a Barbie doll and is a bloody nuisance.'

She was glad enough to slip back into banter and she quipped, 'Am I a bloody nuisance?'

He grinned. 'Looking out for you is my bounden duty.'

Ahead of them several cars had their indicators flashing as they turned into the forecourt of the Lavender Lodge Country Club, which had once been a very large private residence. Restyled and refurbished, with a reputation for good food and first-class sports facilities, it was now an in-place for meeting friends among Clancy's set.

Tonight every window was blazing with light. Music and voices floated across, and the car park was filling. She could hardly have chosen a more public setting to air the split between herself and Hugh. The young couple in a nearby car knew her well. As Clancy got out the girl called, 'Hi, Clancy—see you,' before linking arms with her companion and heading for the club entrance.

Fergus said, 'You are sure about this? You'll be playing under a spotlight.'

'I'll be fine,' Clancy said.

He was in black: shirt, jacket, pants. When he uncoiled from behind the wheel and came round to her she said, 'Black and white. We're colour coordinated.'

'Brilliant. I don't know how we do it.' When the door of the club opened the sound-level rose. 'Half the county seems to be in there,' he said.

She had a flash of panic, then she shrugged. 'Why should I worry? I've got myself a guardian angel.'

But the sardonic face was so far from angelic that

she started laughing. 'I was wrong. A guardian angel is not what I've got. On the contrary.'

'They called the other lot familiars.'

'Are you my familiar?'

He leered. 'Given half the chance.' And that kept her smiling up to the club and through the doors into the entrance hall.

She saw Hugh at once, and he came striding towards her, very much at his ease in this club where he was a valued big-spender.

He was sure that Clancy would come round in the end. His inborn confidence rarely failed him, and he walked through the chattering groups in the entrance hall like a man at home and in charge.

'Good grief,' Fergus muttered. 'He thinks he's lord of the manor.'

'He could be if he wanted,' Clancy whispered back. 'His is a very successful law firm.'

'I'll know where to come if I need a lawyer,' said Fergus. Then, as Hugh reached them, with a warm smile for Clancy and a slightly cooler one for Fergus, 'On second thoughts, perhaps not.'

Hugh had suspected that McKenzie might be with her. He was not going to let that faze him. He said graciously, 'Let me sign you in.'

'That's very civil of you,' said Fergus, as though Hugh really were the host. Clancy wondered if Hugh knew Fergus was laughing at him and thought it was unlikely Hugh would recognise that kind of deadpan mockery.

A smiling manager was welcoming Fergus on Hugh's say-so, as Hugh's guest. Then he repeated the name. '*The* Fergus McKenzie?'

He knows him, Clancy thought, and began to feel

very stupid, because it seemed that several of them had heard of Fergus McKenzie. Some of them had seen articles, a book, TV news appearances. There were little ripples of excitement. Among the familiar faces a newcomer was interesting, and a minor celebrity gave added spice. He was asked what he was doing here and he said he was staying at the old mill house, writing a series of his war-zone assignments. Then a woman who had known her for years asked archly, 'How long have you and Clancy known each other?'

'Clancy and I are very good friends,' said Fergus, and of course he knew what they would make of the oldest cliché in the book. Clancy stood there, trying to act blasé, while Bruce, the manager, suggested Fergus might consider taking out temporary membership. Fergus said he would like to see around.

'I'll show you,' Clancy offered. She got him out of the entrance hall, then strode along the corridor towards the gymnasium. Before they reached it she said, 'I didn't know you were famous.'

'I'm not.'

'You were practically mobbed.'

'A few heads turned,' he said, and she was suddenly sure that before long he would be very well known. The fire was in him, and the power.

She checked her stride, looking at him with startled eyes. 'You're an eye-opener. I didn't know—'

'There's nothing to know. Unless you want Hugh to join us, we'd better keep moving, because he doesn't trust you with me.'

'You don't really want to join this club, do you?'

'I'm not much for clubs.'

But they went on with the pantomime of Clancy

showing Fergus what a smashing set-up the Lavender
Lodge Country Club was. 'Very impressive,' he said,
peering into the well-equipped gym. Passing the tennis
and squash courts, he asked, 'Do you play?' She did.
'Hugh does, of course,' he said.

'He's the club champion,' she boasted, on Hugh's
behalf.

Fergus grinned. 'I must give him a game before I
leave here.'

She would see to it that he didn't get the chance.
There were limits to the mayhem Fergus could leave
behind. It did not occur to Clancy until later that even
with a gammy leg she was assuming that Fergus would
win.

The swimming pool had enough late-night swim-
mers to create waves and a babel of voices. In other
circumstances Clancy might have been among them.
She said, 'The pool's worth the membership fee,' as
they looked in through long windows.

'Your mother said you were a good swimmer.'

'I'm a strong swimmer. That's why she couldn't
understand why I couldn't get out of the river.'

She tried to hide a shudder, but when he said, very
solemnly, 'It was the boots that did it,' she managed
to smile instead.

A man dived from the high board, making a big
splash. She had always loved the brief rush of air and
then cleaving into cold deep water. She had never felt
any fear and she fervently hoped her near-drowning
was not going to spoil it for her.

She turned away from the pool towards Fergus. 'I'm
starving. Shall we try the buffet?'

She took him up a side staircase along a short corridor to a gallery overlooking the restaurant. From up

here you could see who was below, and a red dress caught her eye, swaying seductively in the middle of the dancers. Clancy gripped the railing and leaned over, making sure before she informed him, 'There's Susan, flinging herself around.'

At that moment Susan threw back her head, looked up at Clancy and waved, threading her way through the throng towards the stairs. She was coming up and she was smiling. Beside Clancy, Fergus said, 'She looks like a woman who doesn't know what she's in for.'

'She doesn't know I know, does she?'

'Is she going to?'

'Oh, yes.' If Susan had kept out of her way Clancy would not have gone searching for her, but she couldn't take this sham of phoney friendship. She waited for Susan to start gushing and hugging her, but Fergus was the one in Susan's sights.

She said hello to Clancy, then turned her full attention on the man and cooed, 'I've been hearing about you.' She sounded as if what she had heard had been exciting but what she was seeing was riveting. 'We could do with some more sexy men,' she said, with a naughty-little-girl grin, and Clancy clenched her hands, or she might have grabbed Susan's shoulders and shaken her even dizzier than she was.

Instead she drawled, 'That doesn't say much for Hugh,' and Susan's grin wavered.

But she recovered at once and giggled. 'I did say some more; we do have a few. So what are you doing with this gorgeous hunk?'

'Hedging my bets,' said Clancy. 'Don't you think I should? You can't have spoken to Hugh since he— how can I put it?—helped you with your lease?'

Susan took a backward step, as if she might dart away. Then she asked shakily, 'What has Hugh been saying?'

'He's been saying sorry a lot,' said Clancy.

'What did he tell you?'

'He didn't need to tell me anything. I came back that morning. I saw you.'

That did for any hope Susan might have had of denying everything. Her spluttered, 'Oh, *hell*,' was followed by, 'What can I *say*? Okay, we shouldn't have, but it was sort of for old times' sake. You know how Hugh used to be. He isn't now, of course. It was just—'

Clancy finished ironically, 'Just one of those things,' and Susan agreed eagerly.

'Yeah, that's all it was. Hugh's sorry and so am I. Really, truly sorry. So couldn't we just forget it? Please?' Susan might have been talking about a minor spat, and Clancy half expected her to pout and lisp, Pretty-please.

She spoke softly and savagely. 'Is that the same dress you took off on the stairs in Hugh's house? Your lucky number? Well, it's not going to pull Hugh again, and you'd be wasting your time stripping off for Fergus. So this is not going to be your night, Susan. Unless you've got somebody else lined up.'

Susan flushed, almost as bright as her dress. She mumbled, 'Yeah, well,' and left them, going back down the stairs, joining the dancers again. If she had been dancing with a partner it wasn't Hugh. Clancy didn't see his fair head but he was probably down there somewhere.

For now she stayed where she was, on the gallery standing close to the rail with Fergus just beside her.

That had been heavy. She had to lighten up and carry on pretending she was enjoying herself. 'Would she have been wasting her time doing a striptease for you?' she teased.

He said, 'Perish the thought. Can you forget it?'

'Not yet. She made me so angry I could have pushed her downstairs.'

He grinned. 'I noticed the clenched fists. I thought you might be about to take a swing at her.'

'You weren't far off,' she admitted ruefully.

'Fair enough. Only while you're pitching into that silly bimbo don't go soft on him.'

'Hugh's getting the big chill,' she pointed out.

'Which can do him nothing but good. Smile for your public.'

'What?' They were conspicuous up here. Club members must be gossiping about them. A good number were looking up at them now. She would have to go down, run the gauntlet, try the buffet, dance, even. If she could not do that she should not have come. She babbled, 'Shall we go for the buffet? It's always good; smoked salmon, tiger prawns, super savouries, and lovely little fruit tarts, strawberries and—'

She was chattering away when she felt his hands on her shoulders, turning her so that they were face to face. When he kissed her it was the lightest pressure, just a brushing of lips. 'You taste of wild strawberries,' he said.

She ran the tip of her tongue between her lips, pretending to taste for herself, joking, 'It's my lipstick,' because the kiss had been meant to make her smile. She said, 'Come on,' and moved towards the staircase.

They went into the room below, hand in hand. He had caught her swinging hand when they were halfway down the stairs or she might not have made such a display of togetherness. The looks they were getting showed that not many were missing the linked fingers, and they had to be wondering how Hugh was taking this.

Another ten minutes, thought Clancy, and we can go. At the buffet they filled a plate each and stood by the window, forking the food and making small-talk. Then someone asked Fergus, 'Are you a friend of Hugh's?'

'You'd better ask him that,' Fergus said.

Hugh had joined the group, and Clancy's heart gave its little leap at the sight of him. 'May I?' he said, and put a hand on her arm. The music was 'their tune', but she did not want to dance with Hugh.

Fergus took her plate from her. Then Fergus said, 'No, you may not,' put both of their plates on a window ledge and whisked her away, leaving Hugh standing.

When she glanced back over her shoulder Hugh looked as though he had been dealt a body-blow, and she was almost as breathless herself.

'Has he had his blood pressure tested lately?' Fergus enquired cheerfully. 'He wants to watch it.'

She had never seen Hugh flushed and furious before, but she had probably never annoyed him before, humiliating him in front of so many friends.

When Fergus took a halting step, making her stumble, she said, 'Can you dance with that leg?'

'I'm not too good with two good ones.' He stopped to lean against a wall. 'And I've had enough of the Lavender Lodge mob for one night. Let's go.'

She was glad to get out. She had intended being

cool and confident tonight, not putting on a show as flamboyant as a cabaret.

For a few miles they drove in silence. Fergus was heading for the mill house, which was fine; she didn't want to go home while her mother might still be up. At last he said, 'Did you want to dance with him?'

'No, but he must have asked them to play our tune and I—well I felt sorry for him. It felt as if I'd slapped his face.'

'As good as that?'

'It's a laugh to you, isn't it? But it isn't to me and you don't know Hugh. You can't understand. Ever since my father died Hugh has been a real support.'

Once started, she was away on all the reasons why Hugh Marshall was a man to admire. Until Fergus snarled, 'For God's sake, shut it.'

She bit her lip and snapped back, 'I apologise for boring you.'

'Yeah, you are boring me. He's perfect. Except for that little lapse of getting caught having it off with Susan. Which you were going to overlook. Next week. Or next month. Meanwhile this is the breathing space you said you wanted, so take some deep breaths and stop whingeing.'

'I don't whinge,' she said indignantly, but she must remember his low boredom threshold; she didn't want him striding out of her life just yet. She took a deep breath and said, 'We didn't even get to finish our supper. How about a Chinese takeaway? We could eat it at the mill, and I promise—not another word about Hugh.'

'If I thought you meant that,' he said, 'I'd make love to you myself.'

'Not a solution,' she said.

'No?' he said cheerfully. 'Well, it might be a complication, and we've got enough of them already.'

They surely had. That kiss on the gallery had hardly been a kiss, but if it had lasted, gone deeper, it might have been explosive. The man who had appointed himself her minder was sexy and cynical, and she would be naive not to expect him to make a pass at her some time. If he did, and if she couldn't talk herself out of it, she would fight like a tiger.

'Which way?' he said.

They were nearing a crossroads, and she said, 'Straight on,' so jerkily that he turned to look at her. She thanked her stars he was no mind-reader, because the image in her mind of her struggling against his advances would have either had him laughing or made him wonder if he had another Angela, convinced she was irresistible, on his hands.

The takeaway was almost empty; it was getting late. Clancy did the ordering; she had been here before. Not with Hugh—although the small pretty girl with the long dark hair knew Clancy was engaged to Hugh Marshall the lawyer, and raised a delicate eyebrow when she saw Fergus. Somebody else who'd like an explanation, Clancy thought, ordering the Wandering Dragon.

They opened the tin foil containers on the big scrubbed-top at the mill house and had another buffet, piling two more plates and a third with meaty bits for Bruno, who rapidly developed a passion for prawn crackers.

Clancy was chewing on cashew nuts and feeding the dog on crackers when her phone rang in her purse.

'Don't you go anywhere without that thing?' Fergus asked.

'When I left it behind that wasn't a big success,' she said wryly. She swallowed her mouthful, dug out the phone and said, 'Hello?'

'Clancy.' Hugh's voice was loud enough to make her hold the phone away from her ear. 'Where are you?'

'At the mill.'

'And he's with you?'

'Yes.'

'Well, of course he is. What were you thinking of tonight? This was between you and me; the whole town didn't have to be in on it. I expected you to show some discretion.'

The word 'discretion' hit a mental funnybone, and she yelped, 'Discretion? You want discretion? The man who doesn't shut a bedroom door, let alone lock it.'

But Hugh was considering no one else's point of view. 'They saw you leave me standing. They saw you clear off with him. Most of them noticed you weren't wearing your ring. I have had a gutful of sympathy. They think you are ditching me.' He roared on, as if it was the final straw, 'and now you're at the mill house with him.'

'You're not coming out here?' She got in before he could slam down the phone, because she was not up to this tirade continuing any longer.

'I am not coming out,' Hugh said emphatically. 'You stay the night with him, if that's how you feel, but if you do we are through. And if he isn't out of your life we're finished. It's him or me. Make up your mind.'

The phone was slammed. Fergus, who had been listening, head bent to catch every word, said, 'It doesn't take much to get him riled. I'd hardly started tonight.'

She squeaked, 'What do you mean, you'd hardly started? What more are you planning?'

He shrugged. 'The question is, what are you doing? Him or me, and the man wants a quick answer. Do I walk?'

'Don't be stupid.' Stupid was the last thing Fergus was, but he should know she couldn't be railroaded like this. 'I'm not taking that kind of ultimatum. We shouldn't have gone to the club, and I'm sorry now that I did, but he isn't the only one to have been made a fool of. He knows I'll go back to him in the end.'

Fergus said, 'So are you staying the night?' She glared, and he said, 'Better not. Unless you want to give him a coronary.'

'You still think it's funny, don't you?'

'It has its moments, but don't let him bully you.'

After a pause she said, 'He isn't a bully.' Hugh had never ordered her about before, never even criticised her. She said, 'I'd better go home. I'll leave you with the washing up.'

'What washing up?'

Bruno had taken the opportunity to get on the table, via a chair, and was busily licking over plates and containers. She said, 'Your problem, I think. If he's sick in the night try to keep him off the bed and the rugs.'

Not much was said in the car. It hurt to have Hugh angry with her. She had been so sure of everything and could hardly believe how much had changed in such a short time. She spoke her thoughts aloud. 'I shouldn't have let you come, stirring up a scandal. This should have stayed a private matter.'

'Too late,' Fergus said, so cheerfully that she would have liked to push him out of the car. 'Once you call up a familiar, it's next to impossible to lose him.'

She almost screamed at him. 'Will you stop it? I can't take any more lousy jokes tonight.' Her eyes were misting. She was not a weeper any more than a whinger, but she seemed to be losing hope that life would ever be simple or happy again.

He drew up in the almost deserted street and ran his thumb lightly along her cheekbone. She squeezed her eyes shut and against her lashes his thumb came away wet. She waited for him to scoff, but he said gently, 'It's going to work out, I promise you,' and she looked up into the darkest eyes she had ever known and almost believed him.

She passed a wretched night. Flaunting Fergus publicly had been tactless, and when he had turned out to be something of a celebrity that had been even more of a snub for Hugh. Hugh deserved grief enough to make him think twice before he took up any other offers 'for old times' sake,' but his pride must have been stripped raw tonight.

When he had phoned her at the mill she had been so angry at the emotional blackmail that she had had no hesitation in telling Fergus she would not stand for it. If she gave way her own pride would be in tatters— but what mattered more? Her pride or her love? She had precipitated a collision course, so maybe she should be limiting the damage. Because, of course, there was no contest. Hugh was her life, while the one thing she knew for sure about Fergus was that before long there would be no place in his life for her.

She slept badly, and when her phone rang early she let it ring on while she sat up groggily and stared at it and decided it was probably Fergus again. He was the one who rose with the dawn, and if he was in a flippant mood she would cut him off, because her own sense of humour was at zero.

'Did I wake you?' Hugh asked.

'Yes. Don't start again.' She shook her head to clear it and knew what she was going to say. 'I won't be dictated to. Right now you have no claim on me. I'll go where I like, with who I like, and I am not being bullied by anybody.'

'I know you're not,' said Hugh. 'You've too much spirit.' He was not threatening this morning; he was apologising. 'I don't know what got into me last night. I lost my temper. I love you, Clancy. I trust you, and I'm going to make sure that you trust me again. I've learned my lesson, I'll never forget what I've learned, so can we at least be friends?'

She said, 'Friends sounds a good start.'

She could tell from Hugh's voice that he was smiling. 'So how about a date tonight?' he said.

'Not tonight.'

He said, 'I love you; I'll call you.'

'Goodbye for now,' she said.

Unless there was a rush on, Bets had weekends off. Clancy usually went into the studio for a few hours on Saturday, and this morning, even after her restless night, she was full of energy as she strolled through the gate in the wall into her secret garden, savouring the fresh morning air, sure that it was going to be a beautiful day in spite of grey skies and a chilly wind. Later she was driving over to call on the old man who had been her father's gardener and the first to encourage her love of gardens.

Her gaze followed the flight of a bird overhead, her

spirits flying as high, until Bruno came crashing through the ferns. This time the dog settled for prancing around wagging its tail rather than knocking her flat, but the welcome was still exuberant. 'How long have you been here?' she demanded of Fergus, who was just behind Bruno.

'About half an hour. Everything all right?'

'Very much so. Do you want coffee?' She opened the studio door. She had off-peak heating in here, so it was warm enough to take off topcoats. She unbuttoned herself out of hers, then filled a percolator and switched it on.

Fergus looked up from her drawing boards and remarked, 'You're sounding smug. Why does that worry me?'

'It's too early for quizzes. I don't know why it should worry you. And I'm not smug, just a little happier than I was last night. Hugh phoned to apologise this morning.'

'Saying sorry again?' Fergus was still looking at her sketch plan, turned away from her so that she couldn't see his expression.

She put mugs by the percolator and watched it bubbling because she wanted to smile while she was explaining. 'He lost his temper, and as soon as he calmed down he knew he shouldn't be making demands when he was the one in the wrong. He's going to prove I can trust him again.' She had to smile now. 'So he's on probation, and if we date we date as friends.'

Fergus said softly, 'For anything up to the first half-hour. Odds are you won't hold off any longer.' She didn't expect Fergus to understand, and when he said, 'What the hell is it?' she told him.

'It's love. It may sound dumb to you, but that's how

it goes. When I'm near Hugh I go weak at the knees.'
He could laugh if he liked; she didn't care. 'Even the
aftershave he wears.' She breathed in, as if she could
catch the aroma of it on the warm air. 'He's always
used it and I've always kept a bottle of it. Sometimes
I've slept with a tissue dabbed with it under my pillow.
Crazy, I know, but that is how love can get you.'

She'd expected him to laugh, but he was not even
smiling, 'In your dreams,' he said, and then, 'What
would it take to wake you up?' He had left the drawing
board and was looking at her with a piercing directness
that made her feel that the door had opened and the
bitter wind was blowing in.

'I'll tell you,' he said, in a low and very even voice,
'what you might see if you were awake. That Hughie-
boy is a lightweight and a womaniser.' She shook her
head, but he drawled, 'You told me he was a womaniser. Susan's proved that he still is.'

'Never again.' Hugh had promised her.

'There speaks the dreamer,' Fergus jeered. 'Next
time your knees start giving way remember what you
saw in the mirror before you hit the deck.'

That was cruel, burning the image into her brain,
and she wailed, 'Why are you *doing* this? You said
yourself that it didn't matter, it shouldn't count.'

He shrugged that off. 'Well, I also said I was taking
this minder business seriously, and I am not impressed
by Hughie. Nor am I sure you haven't been brain-
washing yourself over the years into believing you
could kiss the ground he walks on.'

He was so far off the mark she could only say, 'I
pity you. It must be horrible to be so cynical.'

'It has its advantages. You get a clearer view with
the blinkers off.'

'What you're getting is a warped view that I can do without. And I can do without a minder.'

'You want us gone?'

Having him here had only caused trouble. She had known it would but she had let him come, and now some reckless streak in her seemed unwilling to let him go. The percolator gave a final belch and she began to pour carefully, giving the scalding liquid all her attention.

Fergus said cheerfully, 'I'd be sorry to leave. I like the mill house; I could work there. And you need not bother about bedclothes; I bought a sleeping bag yesterday.'

'Sorry, I forgot.' She was actually apologising to him. A minute ago she had hated him, but if she closed her mind to what he had been saying she could probably cope with him being around.

She filled a second mug and took a sip. 'You are a menace,' she said. 'You rock the boat for the hell of it. You wouldn't be messing my love life up to make a pass at me yourself, would you?' She pulled a face, as if the idea were absurd, but she did wonder.

He was all injured innocence. 'The last thing I need is more emotional clutter. I would quite like to stay until you're sure your life is back on track, but you need have no fear that I might try to seduce you.'

He did not look harmless but then he never had. He sounded serious, and she said, 'That is very reassuring.'

'It was meant to be.'

She knew it was meant to reassure her, but she was not at all sure how far she could trust him.

CHAPTER SIX

'WHAT'S going *on*?' was the first thing her mother said when Clancy got back home that night. 'I've been trying to reach you all day.' Clancy had switched off her mobile as they left the mill. 'There've been calls coming through here for you. Where *were* you?'

Clancy said, 'I went to see old Bob.'

Now in his late eighties, their old gardener had long retired to live with his daughter and son-in-law, and Clancy's mother wasn't interested in that.

'And what were you doing last night?' Esta screeched. 'I've had calls asking me if you and Hugh have split up because you were all over this McKenzie man. Margaret Young said you were *kissing* him in front of everybody.'

It *had* got around. Her mother looked as shaken as if she had weathered an earth tremor. 'What did you think you were doing? This isn't like you at all. You must have had a brainstorm. Oh, *poor* Hugh. I rang him and he said I mustn't worry, you'd had a disagreement. But you never quarrel. How could you quarrel with Hugh? You don't know how lucky you are to have Hugh; everybody says so.'

Not everybody thought Clancy wryly. Not Fergus.

'Oh, you *silly* girl.' Now her mother was scolding her as though she was a naughty child. Clancy hung her coat in the little cloakroom off the hall and went into the drawing room, her mother at her heels insisting that she should get on that phone and apologise to Hugh. 'You must have hurt his feelings terribly.'

Clancy had had enough of poor-Hugh, and she said tartly, 'Susan Hines was one of Hugh's old flames, wasn't she?'

That change of topic threw Esta, so that she blinked and said, 'Yes?' Then she smiled fondly. 'She could have been; he always was a heartbreaker. Why?'

'While I was away he and Susan got together again,' said Clancy. 'And the get-together was in bed.'

Esta sat down, feeling for the arms of the chair for support, then clapping a hand over her mouth, gasping, 'Oh, dear. Oh, that was—oh, I'm sure this is one of Susan's stories. I can't believe it of Hugh. I won't believe it. Who told you this?'

'Mother, I saw them.' Clancy knew that her mother wanted to say no. That Clancy had to be mistaken. This could not have happened.

Now Esta put hands over her ears, moaning, 'I don't want to hear any more.' There was no reason why she should, but what Clancy had already told her was enough to reduce her to a wreck.

Hugh—and Hugh's father, until he'd died a few years after Clancy's own father—had always been there for Esta and Clancy. Hugh marrying Clancy had seemed so right. But now Esta was being told that Hugh had let Clancy down, and Clancy was angry, and everything that had been perfect was turning ugly.

The shock brought a panic that had her shaking and Clancy pouring a stiff brandy. At first Esta clenched her teeth and shook her head, but eventually Clancy got her to swallow a little. Then she poured another, which brought the tears flowing, while Clancy sat on the arm of the chair, one of her arms round her mother.

This might not be the best first-aid treatment, but sober Esta was getting hysterical. The brandy was quietening her, so that she let Clancy help her undress and put her to bed. She was asleep when Clancy looked into the room ten minutes later.

In her own room, Clancy got ready for bed. It had been a cheerful day until now. As a young man old Bob had been a Desert Rat with the Eighth Army, and he had told Fergus wartime tales that Clancy had never heard, had shown him medals. They had stayed there all day, and when they'd left Bob's daughter had said, 'You will come again, won't you? You've done him a power of good.' She hadn't been speaking to Clancy, she knew Clancy was a regular visitor, it had been Fergus she was inviting.

Clancy could have gone comfortably to bed without that scene with her mother. The brandy had put Esta to sleep but she would probably wake with a hangover.

Clancy sat at her dressing table in pyjamas, dabbing nightcream on her face. She was churned up herself. Her fingers were shaking, so that she nearly put a blob of cream in her eye, and she opened a drawer for a tissue. An almost full bottle of Hugh's cologne was in the drawer. When she'd told Fergus how sometimes she had slept with a cologne-dabbed tissue under her pillow he'd thought she was behaving like a schoolgirl with a crush. But it was a pleasant aroma. Its potency was because Hugh used it, of course, but she thought she would have liked it anyway.

She unscrewed the cap to sniff it and the bottle slid through her slippery fingers, smashing onto the edge of a heavy cut-glass ashtray.

The ashtray held rings and earrings, and was awash with the liquid, while the dressing table top was splashed and Clancy was drenched. The darn thing had as good as exploded, leaving slivers of glass everywhere.

It took her ages to clear up, and then she had to change her nightgear, sponging herself down to get rid of the smell and the stickiness, and by the time she fell into bed she had gone right off Hugh's cologne.

When she woke it was morning. She lay still, expecting a headache, although she rarely suffered headaches, and then she remembered last night's drama and the brandy she had poured for her mother. It was her mother who would have the headache, and Clancy must be on hand with coffee and aspirins.

But Esta had provided her own coffee. When Clancy came down her mother was sitting at the kitchen table in her blue housecoat, with an empty coffee cup, looking a little paler than usual but with her blonde hair smooth and a touch of lipstick.

Before Clancy could get out How are you? Esta was asking, 'What did Hugh have to say about all this?'

'That it just happened once and never will again.'

Esta nodded approvingly, as if that was the right answer, and asked her next question, 'Are you still engaged?'

Clancy muttered something non-committal and her mother persisted, 'But you are going to marry him?'

'Well, yes.'

Her mother's face softened as she reached across the table to pat Clancy's hand. 'You two were meant for each other. Your father used to say that. Remember when you were very young and he used to tease you about how you idolised Hugh?'

Clancy remembered how she would blush and deny

it and her father would say that nobody was good enough for his princess but Hugh was all right.

'He would have been so happy when Hugh asked you to marry him,' her mother said dreamily, and Clancy knew how it would have pleased her father. Then Esta gave a woman-of-the-world shrug. 'Well, of course I've very disappointed in Hugh, but he is a man and these things do happen, and while you're getting your own back, flirting with somebody else, you could be losing him.'

'I need to feel I can trust him again.'

'Of *course* you do.' Her mother couldn't agree more. 'But what I'm saying is, don't take too long about it, because Susan Hines isn't the only one ready to catch Hugh on the rebound.'

'I'll remember that,' Clancy said dryly.

Her mother pushed back her chair and stood up. 'I'll get dressed.'

A few seconds later, as she was filling the kettle, Clancy heard her mother on the phone in the hall. 'You get round here, young man. I want a word with you.'

She almost dropped the kettle, rushing into the hall where her mother was replacing the phone. She couldn't have been calling Fergus; she didn't know his number. It had to have been Hugh. She was getting Hugh over for a family conference.

'I don't want Hugh here,' Clancy howled.

She grabbed the phone and punched Hugh's number, which rang on. Either he was not taking calls or he had answered Esta's summons like greased lightning. She went out of the house into the driveway to get to Hugh's car as soon as he arrived, and because she could not trust herself not to start screaming at her mother. Stop interfering. Leave us alone.

Hugh arrived, as if he had had his foot on the accelerator all the way, and Clancy's idea of sending him home again was scuppered by Esta in the doorway, beckoning him into the house. As he got out of the car Clancy hissed, 'This is ridiculous.'

'You told her about Susan?'

'I didn't see why I should be the one blamed for everything.'

'How's she taking it?'

Having beckoned him in, Esta had retreated into the house again. Clancy said, 'She was hysterical last night. This morning she's Mrs Fix-it, putting everything right.'

'I'm with her there,' said Hugh. And she is with you, Clancy thought bitterly.

Esta was sitting in her usual rosewood armchair in the drawing room. She raised a tragic face and asked huskily, 'Hugh, how could you?'

'I honestly don't know.' Hugh's voice matched her mother's. They both sounded as if they had laryngitis. Hugh could hardly croak the words out. 'I can't start to tell you how sorry I am. If I thought I'd lost you two I wouldn't have much left to live for. You're my family; you mean everything to me.'

Clancy could imagine Fergus listening with a raised eyebrow, saying, Sorry again.

Because Hugh *was* saying sorry again. 'I'm so sorry,' Hugh was saying. 'I swear I can't envisage going on alone without Clancy.'

Her mother, still hurt but forgiving, was telling him, 'There is no reason why you should.' As if Clancy had no say in the matter and they were settling this between them.

Now Hugh was telling her mother, 'I'm going to do everything to win back her love and her forgiveness,' and Clancy knew he believed everything would be forgiven before long. She could smell his cologne, although that was probably still in her nostrils after last night, and it had lost most of its magic. 'Clancy, will you come with me? Please?' he asked winningly and hopefully.

If she went they would find somewhere for lunch and then for a romantic dinner for two while Hugh used his charm to beguile her. He and her mother had the same almost happy faces, and now she could imagine Fergus drawling, They're a gang of two and you're the one getting mugged. Get out of there.

She said, *'No,'* so sharply that her mother frowned, hope replaced by annoyance that Clancy was being so obstinate.

Hugh's boyish face crumpled before he made a brave effort to smile at Esta, asking her, 'May I still come round here, or am I banned?'

'You have always been welcome in our home,' said Clancy's mother sweetly. 'I hope you always will be.'

'I'm off,' said Clancy.

Hugh said, 'Come back.'

He meant come back to him, and her mother said, 'She will.'

'Don't answer for me,' said Clancy. 'Don't tell each other what I'm going to do.'

She was so near to losing her temper that she could have blown an argument, and she didn't wait for one. She drove with the car windows open to cool herself down, but she was still seething when she reached the mill house. She had guessed whose side her mother would be on, but she need not have forgiven Hugh with open arms in the first five minutes.

She rapped on the door of the mill house and opened it, calling, 'Hi, are you at home?' His car was outside, he wouldn't be far, and Bruno came through the door that led off the living room into what had been the working mill.

Fergus was in there, standing in the shadowy high-vaulted area with its feeling of dampness, emptiness, although some of the equipment, including the great millstones, was still in place.

He turned and smiled at her, and right away she felt better—enough to begin explaining what was what in here. What she had inherited when she bought the mill, what she had acquired over the years.

'It could be a working mill again. We could start grinding flour once the wheel's turning. We need cogs and bearings and a specialist builder, of course. I'm hoping to do it next year, with the rest of my trust fund.' Above her head Fergus sniffed, and she put a hand up, 'Is it my hair? Did I get it in my hair?'

He breathed deeper. 'What are you talking about?'

'That cologne of Hugh's. I dropped the bottle of it last night and it smashed all over the place. I was drenched and my dressing table top was swimming in it.'

He grinned. 'Did it send you weak in the head?'

'No, it didn't. Half a litre of it turns your stomach.'

'But this was the magic potion?'

His arms were around her, his face was against her hair, and she could feel a heart thumping that might have been his but was much more likely to be her own. Again she got that sensation of comfort and reassurance from being close to him. And something else, like a faint warning bell, that made her lift her head and start talking.

'My mother phoned Hugh this morning and asked him round home, so that we could kiss and make up. He said sorry again and they both thought that was enough.'

'What did you do?'

'I walked out and came here. They were ganging up against me.' She rolled her eyes. 'My mother thinks that Hugh might have made a silly mistake with Susan but if I don't sweeten up fast one of his old girlfriends is going to nab him.'

'Lining up for him, are they?'

'My mother thinks so, and she could be right.'

'Doesn't strike me as a woman who's right about much,' said Fergus. 'And if somebody else does get him it won't be your loss. You're too good for the pair of them.'

It wasn't true. Her mother was a good woman and Hugh was the man she loved, but it was flattering to be told, for once, that she hadn't been the only lucky one when Hugh put the ring on her finger.

Fergus could boost her ego, making her feel sexy and sassy. He was no longer holding her but she was getting the vibes as if she were still in his arms, his lips on her throat, on her lips. She could stand away from him and still be in a magnetic field—which had to be warning her what lunacy sex with no holding back would be.

Nothing would be worth the havoc it could make of her life. No way was she playing with this fire.

His laptop was on the table, with an open file, papers and notebooks. 'Tomorrow will do,' he said. 'Have you had breakfast?'

'I've had no time for anything. She was up and about when I got downstairs, determined to get Hugh and me together again. She's got a will of iron, my mother.'

'Another bully.' He took two slices from a wrapped ready-cut loaf on the dresser, lit the grill on the stove and put them under. 'Which is why you need your eyes wide open before they get you stitched up again.'

'I know what I'm doing.'

'Let us hope so,' he said.

She ate the toast and drank a cup of instant coffee while he closed down the computer and filed the papers. Then they got into her Transit van and drove away from the mill, through the high street of the village.

The bells were ringing as churchgoers headed for early-morning service. Some of them Clancy knew. When she stopped at traffic lights the driver and passenger in a car beside her waved. She recognised a couple of familiar faces and saw them peering at Fergus where they might have expected Hugh to be.

The lights turned green, the cars went separate ways, and she said to Fergus, 'Those two could be wondering if we're running away together.'

'We are. Shall we go back to the Fisherman's Rest?' But there could be no going back to the little inn, any more than you could change the past. She only wished she could.

'Penny for them,' said Fergus. She was looking thoughtful and she had just sighed.

She said, 'I was wishing I *could* go back. Just to after I came home, because I shouldn't have advertised

to everybody that Hugh and I have hit a sticky patch.
I shouldn't have let you come.'

He said cheerfully, 'What makes you think you
could have kept me away?'

There was no use arguing about that. Nor in regretting where she had gone wrong.

'Where *are* we going?' Fergus asked.

'This is a mystery tour. If you see anywhere that
takes your fancy, do speak up.'

He fiddled with the lever to push his seat farther
back—more space for his long legs—and settled himself comfortably. 'I'll leave it to you,' he said. 'As
long as we get away from your friends. I'm starting
to feel like a zoo exhibit.'

She laughed at that, but made no cracks. Then she
turned on the radio, finding a popular music pro-
gramme, easy listening, and they covered a few more
miles, keeping out of towns, staying in rural areas,
before she slowed down and Fergus looked up. She
said, 'We've just passed a garage sale.'

'And?'

'That's one of the ways I'm furnishing the mill
house. You never know what you might find. Do you
mind?'

'I'm for anything that's for the mill house,' he said
approvingly. 'Let's go.'

On the pavement he took her arm and they saun-
tered together towards the driveway, the open garage
and the spread of goods on offer.

She always enjoyed picking up bargains for the mill
house, but with Fergus the fun had an added sparkle.
The girl running the sale thought they were a smash-
ing-looking couple buying for a home where they
lived together. In a way they *were* sharing a home,

they both had a stake in the mill house right now, and when Clancy was undecided about a wicker table and two chairs Fergus said, 'Have them. They're just the thing for a summer evening.'

She could imagine sitting outside in the sunshine, with long cool glasses, talking, smiling with somebody who, come summer, was unlikely to be Fergus. But it was him she was seeing, and she said, 'Why not? They can go in a spare room till summer.'

It was a carefree day. A garage sale, then a Sunday market the girl had told them about on the old airfield. It could have been humdrum, but never was for a moment.

With Bruno on a lead they went on a cheap and cheerful spending spree among the crowds and the stalls and the dealers, half filling the little van.

They had lunch at a pub, watching a darts match, and dinner in a classy restaurant with the decor of a French château and a menu that described mouth-watering dishes and nearly lived up to its promise.

Here they shared an elaborate fish platter with a cream and lemon dip and talked about what they had stacked up in the van and where she would put it in the mill house. And about the week ahead of her.

Now the day was nearly over she had to start thinking about tomorrow. She was consultant for a roof garden for a block of flats and was meeting an engineer, to assess the lead-bearing capacity, and someone from the local council in case planning permission was needed. Another day she was spending with the couple who wanted her to design a garden on the plot of their newly built house, to get to know them and hear about their dreams.

'All systems go,' said Fergus.

'Uh-huh. While I'm working I shall be okay. Getting through the bits between could be tougher.'

'Don't let them grind you down,' he said. 'Are we going back tonight?'

It would have been fantastic to have asked for a room and stayed here being amused and cosseted as she had been all day. Forgetting till morning everything and everybody outside the walls of the bedroom and the unimaginable possibilities of the bed.

'You know darn well we're going back,' she said.

After they'd unloaded the van and got the booty into the house they still had to manoeuvre it into place. Fergus still had a groggy leg, although the rest of him was in peak condition, and when he groaned, shouldering a chest of drawers up the staircase, Clancy howled, 'I told you so. Leave it down here or let me do it.'

He said, 'Shut up or I'll drop it on you.'

'What you need,' she said, 'is a minder.'

The chest of drawers went up, and so did the put-u-up bed, and with the day's buys spread around the house looked a little less bleak and a little more lived-in.

She said, 'It's lovely. I have had a super day.'

'So have I.' She believed him. By his standard it had hardly been exciting, and it might not be the kind of day he would want again. But he had not been bored; she was sure of that.

He had paid for most of this. The prices had mostly been peanuts, but he was living here rent-free, and when she'd protested over the chest of drawers at twenty-five pounds he'd said, 'I've got to leave you something to remember me by.'

'Oh, I'll remember you,' she'd said.

Now she said, 'Thank you.'

'Thank you,' he said. 'Give my love to your mother.'

She was home before midnight. They had spent some time unloading her van and putting her purchases in place. It had been fun, buying for her mill house at knockdown prices. The rugs, the wicker furniture, a wall mirror and the put-u-up bed meant that she had made a start in one of her upstairs rooms.

Her mother came into the hall as Clancy came into the house, sighed deeply and said plaintively, 'Well, you didn't stay out all night; that's something to be thankful for. I've been worrying myself sick waiting for you.'

Clancy pretended to be puzzled. 'Did you think I might have crashed the van?'

'Don't be so smart,' Esta snapped.

'Ah, we're talking about *sex*,' Clancy said. 'But that's all right because I wasn't away all night. Well, Hugh and Susan could have told you there's no law against sex by daylight.'

As she went upstairs she heard her mother spluttering below, too exasperated to bother any more with Clancy tonight.

Hugh's photograph was back on her bedside table. Her mother must have searched for it and replaced it. Clancy picked it up. Fergus would shrug and say, I told you he was a lightweight. Doesn't he look it? And for the first time she began to consider if Hugh's good looks were rather immature. She put the photograph back in her case, locking it, hoping her mother would get the message without needing it spelled out.

She was glad of her workload that week, because her social life was stressful. All their friends seemed

to have had Clancy and Hugh down as the couple
bound to make a match. Hugh had got around, Clancy
was pretty and popular, but their engagement had been
nothing like the shock of their split.

Everybody in their circle had heard how Clancy had
caught Hugh with Susan Hines. There was plenty of
gossip and a fair amount of sniggering and everyone
wanted to know what was happening now.

Clancy's new friend was a knockout, although they
were only supposed to be friends. And she was supposed to have lost her ring, but those who raised the
subject with Hugh got short shrift. They went on tittle-
tattling behind his back. Rumours got around that
Clancy was continuing to make him sweat.

Her women-friends had less compunction about being curious, which was why she kept out of their way
as much as possible, only admitting that, yes, she and
Hugh had a problem they were trying to get round.
But even her closest friends were enjoying the spicy
little scandal.

Hugh was behaving well, considering how he must
resent becoming a laughing stock. He rang a couple
of times, but when Clancy turned down his suggestion
that they should meet he sighed and said he could
wait.

Work filled her days, but she did spend some time
with Fergus that week. Tuesday evening they went to
a cinema, catching a film Clancy had wanted to see.
It had been described as 'a riot of laughter', and it was
funny enough to keep the audience chuckling most of
the time. Although after the first hour the joke began
wearing thin for Clancy.

In all the seats around her couples seemed to be
very much together, while she was sitting stiffly, keep-

ing her distance from Fergus, who was lounging beside her.

She knew it was stupid. How could it have mattered if she had relaxed enough to put her head on his shoulder? But she wouldn't let herself risk it, and she wondered if he noticed that her body-language was so uptight.

If he did it would be amusing him, but when he touched her arm he said, 'Would you mind if we got out? My leg's playing up.'

The seating was cramped. The cinema was not called the Bijou for nothing. With his height leg space would have been constricted even if he had been able to adjust, and Clancy jumped up, murmuring, 'Excuse me' as they stumbled over feet along the row to the exit.

'Are you all right?' she asked.

He looked all right. 'Sure,' he said. 'Sorry you missed the film.'

'I saw enough.'

There was a theatre bar next door to the cinema. He suggested, 'Shall we go in here?' and they settled with coffee and ham on rye sandwiches and Clancy relaxed.

Until she saw the couple who were coming in. Then she groaned, 'Aw, heck.'

They were spotted, of course. The dapper little man and the fussy little woman prided themselves on never missing a trick and they made straight for Clancy and Fergus.

'Who are they?' he asked, watching them approach.

'The nosiest pair in town. Nothing is going to stop them grilling us for all the juicy details.'

'What juicy details? Two friends having coffee?'

'I don't want them told anything,' she said, through gritted teeth.

They knew about Hugh and they were sizing up Fergus. Clancy was sure that Wynne at least would soon suss out that Clancy fancied Fergus rotten.

She wished she could walk, but the sandwiches had only just been served. And Wynne, eyes twinkling, was asking, 'May we join you, or do you want to be alone?'

They edged in and sat down, smiling, and Clancy did sketchy introductions. 'Wynne and Gerald Whitehouse, Fergus McKenzie.'

'Ah, the journalist,' said Gerald, also twinkling. 'And how long has this been going on?'

'A while,' said Fergus. 'What's your line of business?'

They had an antiques shop and he leaned forward, chin in hand. 'That must be interesting,' he said, and right away he had them discussing antiques, recalling outsmarting other dealers, talking about themselves.

He was knowledgeable and charming and Clancy knew they would say later What an intelligent young man, although they hadn't asked any of the personal questions they had intended to ask.

At last Fergus said, 'We must be going.'

'How's Hugh these days?' Wynne got in.

'Ask him,' said Clancy, gathering up her handbag.

They would be coming across others who were determined to pry, and Fergus wouldn't be able to hold them all off, but on Thursday night they went to the theatre and got away with someone waving at them from a box.

There was much more leg-room in the theatre seats, and the play was gripping. The suicidal Anna

Karenina going mad from love betrayed. Clancy came out of the performance feeling slightly punch-drunk. 'What a carry-on,' said Fergus, and they discussed the play and the players most of the way to her home.

When he drew the car up outside Clancy said, 'Come in for another coffee.'

Her mother was not going to welcome him, but it was Clancy's home and Esta's antagonisms would not bother Fergus.

He accepted without hesitating. Esta's greeting was chilly. While Clancy fixed coffee in the kitchen her mother was left with Fergus in the drawing room.

Esta spoke about the weather and the play like royalty making small-talk, and as Clancy was pouring she left the room, coming back with a red-leather-bound album. She seated herself by Fergus. 'Would you like to see some photographs of Clancy?' she said.

'Yes, I would.'

Clancy spluttered a protest but her mother had opened the book. More than half the snapshots were of Hugh, which was why Esta had produced it. She was showing Hugh off. Affluent, handsome, brilliant Hugh. How about this for competition? she was saying to Fergus. What can you offer my daughter to equal this?

She turned page after page for Fergus, who thought the whole performance was hilarious although he kept a straight face, making appreciative sounds. When Esta started telling him what a successful lawyer Hugh was, Fergus said solemnly, 'The man is an inspiration.'

Clancy leaned across and closed the album. 'I think you've had enough,' she said.

'He takes a splendid photograph,' said Fergus. 'Es-

pecially on horseback. You could put him in a cata-
logue any day.'

'Shouldn't you be going?' said Clancy. Outside, as
she walked him to his car, she apologised. 'You must
have found that dead boring. She's doing the proud
mother. Hugh's mother. She isn't so proud of me.
Some of it was you, some was to remind me how
wonderful Hugh is.'

'Yup,' said Fergus. 'But we all know that.' He un-
locked his car door and got in. 'Everything's come so
easily to him,' he said. 'Makes you wonder how he'd
be if he hit hard times.'

Clancy had given Hugh a fairly hard time, but when
he phoned on Friday morning and asked, 'Will you be
taking McKenzie to the club again tonight?'

'Once was enough,' she said.

'More than enough,' said Hugh, and she didn't see
how she could disagree there.

Hugh had caught her getting ready to leave the
house, checking papers in her briefcase with the phone
tucked into her shoulder.

His voice dropped to an intimate low. 'Is it too soon
to suggest again that we might have an evening by
ourselves? Please, Clancy. Let's get together again.'

Less than a week's probation wasn't much; but if
she and Hugh were seen around together they
wouldn't be news any more; it would scotch most of
the rumours. She gave way. 'I'll be home any time
after half-six.'

He erupted with relief. 'Oh, thank you, bless you.
Oh, my darling, I love you.'

She wasn't echoing, I love you, as she'd used to.

She said, 'I must fly. I've got a date with a steel girder.'

She was busy all day, but before she went home she drove round to the mill house to tell Fergus what she was doing. It seemed fair enough, keeping him posted. She would not be discussing it. She would just be telling him that she was going out with Hugh tonight, no big deal, but they might start to put the Susan affair behind them. And if Fergus still felt an urge to rock the boat he could get out of the mill house and find himself another bolt-hole.

His car was not parked outside the mill house. This car had a woman at the wheel, who wound down the window as Clancy drew up and called, 'Do you know where Fergus is?' as Clancy opened her door.

Clancy said, 'If he isn't in, I don't. Who are you?'

'That's what I was going to ask you.'

The woman got out of her car, huddled into a long pale beige fur coat, and even if it was fake it must have cost a packet. She was waiting for Clancy to speak, so Clancy said, 'I own this place. I'm Clancy Lindhurst.'

'Yes, of course.' She sounded as if she knew that. 'Well, I'm Angela Denby.'

Clancy had thought she might be. 'Is he expecting you?' she asked.

'But of course. Didn't he tell you I was coming?'

What Fergus had told Clancy about a girl called Angela was that she was a bloody nuisance, but this was a girl any man would be proud to have on his arm. Her face was exquisitely pretty, with creamy skin and huge dark eyes. Her voice was breathless, almost whispering. 'Can we go inside? It's cold out here.'

This was Fergus's problem. It was up to him to deal

with it. Clancy could hardly leave her outside, shivering in her lush coat.

But she opened the door reluctantly to let Angela Denby follow her into the mill house. She was more than irritated, wanting to tell this woman to get lost, as though she was somebody Clancy disliked intensely.

She sat down, her coat like a cloud around her, and Clancy said automatically, 'Can I get you anything? A drink?'

There was an opened bottle of red wine on the table. 'I'll have a glass of that,' she said, and Clancy washed the glass on the draining board and wondered where Fergus was and what he would say when he walked in here. She had to ask. 'When did he ask you to come down here?'

'What has he been telling you about me?' asked Angela.

'That he and your partner worked together.'

'What else?' Angela sat very still, her huge eyes unblinking.

That after her partner had been killed Angela had decided that Fergus should take his place with her. He had not been flattered or interested, he had told Clancy. That was what he had said, but Clancy could hardly repeat that. 'Nothing else,' she said.

'He didn't tell you about the baby?'

Clancy's mouth went dry. 'What baby?'

'Ours,' said Angela. 'Mine and Fergus's.'

CHAPTER SEVEN

CLANCY'S convulsive jerk of shock snapped the stem of the wineglass between her fingers.

The crack made a sharp report, and Angela said softly, 'You've fallen for him, haven't you? Oh, poor Clancy. Oh, I am sorry. I'm not surprised, but don't expect it to lead to anything.'

Clancy looked at her fingers; there was no blood on them. The glass lay in two pieces on the table and she dropped them into a trash bucket. This was staggering, after what Fergus had told her, but Angela was making one big mistake. Clancy's relationship with Fergus was platonic. All the eroticism had been in her head. Physically she had known they were not leading anywhere. But she would rather not be here when he got back, because this could be embarrassing, and although she was quite composed she had to get away.

She took another glass from a cupboard and poured wine carefully, offering the glass to Angela, who sipped and smiled. 'Too dry for me, but it's how he likes it.'

'Is it?'

'I do know him better than you,' said Angela. 'We've been lovers for over a year.'

The word slipped out. 'Before—?' And Angela took that up quickly.

'Before Alan was killed? Oh, long before then. I used to think it was because neither of us wanted to hurt Alan that Fergus insisted on keeping it from him, but afterwards, when there was nothing standing in our way, he made it very clear he was not into commitment.'

Her eyes met Clancy's in what was surely a clear and candid gaze. She said, 'And, yes, the affairs is still very much on. He's a fabulous lover and so am I. He can't do without me for long, and I do know that nobody else stands a chance with him.'

Clancy said, 'That's nice for you. Make yourself at home. He shouldn't be long.'

'Any message?' asked Angela.

'Nothing that won't wait,' said Clancy.

She drove away from the mill, hoping she would not pass Fergus's car because she had to get her head cleared before she saw him again. She couldn't think straight, let alone talk straight. She had to concentrate to drive safely, as though her motor neurone system had gone haywire.

She drew up off the road at the side of a farm track and sat, staring ahead and seeing nothing. A baby. Angela had said there was a baby. Was she pregnant now, under that swaddling coat, or was there a son or a daughter? Had they been cheating on Fergus's friend, her partner, before Alan was killed? If Angela was lying it was a tacky tale, but it could be true. She could easily know him better than Clancy because there was not that much about him that Clancy did know.

But why was the shock so violent that Clancy had walked out of the mill house traumatised? Why did it matter so much? Because Fergus mattered to her. She *was* falling for him. Not in a little way, but heading for a killer of a fall. Finding Angela waiting for him at the mill house couldn't have maddened her more if she *had* been having a physical affair with Fergus that Angela was here to destroy. And further back, with Susan. On the gallery at the club that wave of rage that had made her nearly push Susan down the stairs had been because she was coming on so blatantly to Fergus. A primitive possessiveness had made Clancy want to say, You can keep your hands off this one; he's mine.

Fergus was not hers. He might be Angela's. Or nobody's. Just his own man. Clancy had no way of knowing whose he was, or who he was, he had given so little away about himself. But she sat huddled in the driving seat of her little van and knew that she was way out of her depth.

It was different with Hugh, who she knew so well, and she was so glad that she had agreed to see Hugh again.

She was safe to drive by now, and she should be going home to change from her business suit into something feminine and flattering. But that would mean listening to her mother, smug as the cat with the cream now that Clancy had 'stopped being silly', so Clancy drove round to Hugh's offices to meet him there.

Marshall and Lindhurst had a first-floor suite in a substantial redbrick Edwardian building in the town centre. It was familiar to Clancy, from when her father had practised there, and although carpets and fittings had been replaced there was still the rich ambience of mahogany panelling and leather-covered desk and chairs. The chambers still looked like the setting of long-established family solicitors, although the old partners had gone. Hugh headed the firm now, his colleagues were fairly recently qualified and Daisy, who had been his father's secretary, could have been a grandmother to the two young secretaries.

Daisy was a little birdlike woman with sharp nose and sharp eyes, hair still black as a raven's wing, and like everyone else in the office she had heard about the trouble between Hugh and Clancy.

She was delighted to see Clancy and ushered her into Hugh's office, closing the door on gossiping juniors before she asked anxiously, 'Is everything all right?'

Clancy smiled. 'Oh, yes, Hugh was collecting me from home but I thought I'd come round here and meet him. He is coming back, is he?'

He was. Any time now. Daisy said roguishly, 'I knew he couldn't afford to let you go,' and Clancy nearly said, I'm not that much of a prize. But it was nice to hear that Daisy thought she was.

Hugh had seen Clancy's van in the car park, so he was prepared for her. She was still in his office with Daisy when he came in, smiling broadly, enveloping Clancy in a bear hug while Daisy tactfully withdrew.

This was their reconciliation. Clancy being held by Hugh in a wordless embrace. She relaxed against him, getting a whiff of his cologne, which was discreet enough but still reminded her of being drenched in the stuff.

'I've booked at the Gateway again, is that okay?' Hugh was asking her.

'Perfect,' she said. 'Do you want to go home and change? I don't. If I do my mother could start reading me the Riot Act.'

Clancy had clothes in a wardrobe in Hugh's bedroom, and she was almost certain she could go in there, blotting out the bad memories, but Hugh said, 'Let's wash and go.'

He was not pushing his luck. Things were going well and would go better before the night ended, but not yet in the bedroom where she had caught him with Susan.

The Gateway was a select and intimate restaurant run by two excellent cooks who recognised Clancy and Hugh as regulars without knowing them personally. They were given a good table, with good service and delicious food, and Clancy told herself she was happy again.

When she looked at Hugh she could pretend this was before she'd set off for that exhibition she had never reached. But over the coffee, when Hugh asked teasingly, 'Shall I buy you a ring to be going on with, or shall we wait till the insurance comes through and get a real replacement?' she was taken back to the Fisherman's Rest.

Now what was she going to say? She had lost the ring in the flooded river. If she kept quiet, presumably the insurance company would pay up, but it would be fraud and Fergus could tell what had really happened. He knew, and so did she, and she blurted, 'It didn't slip off my hand when I fell in. I threw it into the water.'

Hugh looked puzzled, then staggered, then he said, 'You...did...what?' pausing between each word.

He had heard, but she repeated it. 'I took it off and dropped it in the river. I was angry.'

She had been light-headed and running a temperature, but it had been madness, and Hugh said in hushed tones, 'Have you any idea what it was worth?'

'I know. I'm sorry.'

She watched him struggling to regain his composure until he managed to say, 'Let's forget it for now. Don't let's spoil tonight.'

She was grateful for a little reprieve. 'Yes, please,' she said, and they both tried to bridge the awkward moment.

Their talk was stilted for a while, but before they left the restaurant they seemed an affectionate item again, and as they drove towards their own town Hugh asked, 'Your place or mine?'

She said, 'Mine. We'd better tell my mother we've been out together.'

'She knows. I rang her earlier.'

Clancy smiled. 'So she'll either be waiting up with the champagne or have taken herself off and left us all alone.'

'It's not champagne I'm wanting,' said Hugh, and she went on smiling.

They called at the parking lot behind his offices for Clancy to collect her van and then drove in a convoy of two to her house. Lights were on, but the only sign of her mother was a note left on the kitchen table: 'I'm having an early night. See you in the morning. Love, Mother.'

Standing behind Clancy, reading the note over her shoulder, Hugh lifted her hair and kissed the back of her neck. She waited for the thrill that she'd always felt. It was longer coming this time but she turned towards him.

They got out of the kitchen into the drawing room, where the carpet was thick. Hugh was fumbling with his dark red silk tie and Clancy began to unbutton her coat with trembling fingers. Her legs were giving way; she would be slithering down on the carpet.

'Before you hit the deck,' Fergus had said, 'remember what you saw in the mirror.' And the image— Hugh and Susan, flushed and sleeping after sex—came back to her in total and terrible recall.

Her spine stiffened and her head snapped back. She gasped, 'Not yet. I'm not ready yet.'

'*What?*' Hugh was as dumbfounded as he had been when she'd told him she'd dumped his ring. 'I can't believe this. This isn't you; you've never been a tease.'

She was not teasing now. She was encountering something that made lovemaking with Hugh impossible. And it was as though a lifeline had been dragged from her, leaving her nothing to cling to as the flotsam of her life swirled past.

Hugh said, 'I'll ring you tomorrow. And get your act together, because I can't be taking much more of this.'

Neither can I, Clancy thought, and I only wish it were an act. She followed him as he left the house and stood watching the lights of his car as he took it out of the drive onto the road.

Beside her Fergus said, 'That didn't last long. I was on my way to the front door when he stormed out.'

She was still in her topcoat and she dug both hands into her pockets, as if she could hold herself together that way. 'What are you doing here?'

'I've been waiting for you. I phoned and got your mother; she told me you were out with Hugh.'

'Why are you stalking me?' she flamed. 'You're no guardian angel. That spell you've put on me is nearer black magic. Telling me to remember what I saw in the mirror. And that's what I did. Before we were even kissing I was seeing them in that horrible mirror. You're inside my head. I keep hearing what you'd be saying and it is sending me round the bend, so how long is this going on?'

'Long enough, I hope,' he said.

'Leave me alone,' she howled. 'Go back to Angela and the baby.'

'*What?*' He grabbed her shoulders, nearly yanking her off her feet. 'What did Angela say to you?'

'Ask her.'

'She told me you let her in then left right away.'

'Not before we talked.'

'So what did she *say*?'

She wanted to run, but under his grip she could only squirm while his eyes looked into hers as if he could probe her mind. She forced the words through her teeth. 'That you'd been lovers long before your mate was killed. You don't want commitment but you're having such fantastic sex together that your affair is still white-hot as ever. That's why you asked her to come down here, because you can't do without her.'

'And you believed this?'

'How am I supposed to know what to believe?' she yelped. 'She probably knows you better than I do. I know what you told me and I know what she told me, but how do I know which of you is lying?'

He said harshly, 'You don't, because you're too stupid to spot a phoney if he came dressed as Father Christmas. And what baby?'

'Hers… Yours.'

He let her go then, throwing his arms wide in furious rejection. 'I give up. I knew you were gullible but you can't have the sense you were born with or you'd have recognised a raving fantasist. She's a natural-born liar, but you couldn't decide who to believe—her or me.'

His voice was biting, and he looked at Clancy as if he had done with her. 'I told you we were never lovers, and sure as hell we are never going to be. There was no baby. There was an abortion about a year ago. Alan's baby. He wanted it, she didn't, and she had the abortion. That's my version. Please yourself which you believe, because frankly I give rather less than a damn.'

He turned to go, and if she hesitated he would be gone for ever. She wasn't hesitating, she was running after him. What she had done was nearly unforgivable. How could she have listened to a stranger's lie? It was because Clancy was falling for Fergus herself that Angela's fantasy had been unbearable, and she had carried on like a jealous idiot.

She couldn't tell him that, but couldn't let him go. Her minder, her friend—whatever he was, she needed him desperately, and she begged, 'Don't be like this. *Please*, I shouldn't have listened to her, but she came at me out of the blue and she said you'd asked her to come, and she looked so fragile and trusting, sitting there shivering in a great coat.'

'Do you believe me?'

'Of course I do.' She chanced a smile, and when he smiled too the relief was enormous. She coaxed, 'Come back to the house. I'll make us a drink.'

'And risk meeting your mother? I rang earlier and she told me you were out with Hughie and wasn't that splendid and all your friends were going to be so happy for you.' He mimicked Esta's glee and Clancy laughed.

'It won't matter much to my friends. Only my mother thinks keeping Hugh and me together is such a mighty deal.'

'What do you think?'

'Well, I suppose it is.' Although tonight had shown her they had been rushing too soon into intimacy.

'We must talk.' Fergus took her arm and she looked up at him enquiringly.

'Talk about what?'

'Problems,' he said. 'Yours and mine.'

Talking about their problems might not solve them, but it was not late and she would rather spend the next hour or so with Fergus than go into the house alone. She said, 'Let's go to the studio.'

The night was cold and still. Moonlight made silvery shadows through the black boughs of the trees, and Clancy let the peace flow over her until they came to the little clearing of the garden house. Then she said, 'I'd have liked a tree house but I needed a working office.'

'A house in the woods is definitely the next best thing.'

It was warmer inside, and she took off her topcoat, draped it over the back of a chair and flopped down into the chair, declaring, 'Since I finished work it's been one jolt after another, what with Angela waiting at the mill, hallucinations about mirrors and a row with you.'

Fergus raised an eyebrow. 'You call that a row? We could do much better than that.'

She grinned. 'You could be right. If we should ever get into a real fight can I choose the weapons?'

'You can choose them; I won't promise to use them.'

They were fooling, and her spirits were rising so that the Angela episode was becoming absurd and she could ask, 'Is she still at the mill house?'

'I did see her off, but I wouldn't put it past her to be sitting outside again when I get back.' Nor would Clancy. 'Something will have to be done about her,' Fergus went on, 'I thought I was handling it, but you're the first she's told this tale and she's airhead enough to start believing it.'

She couldn't resist a touch of mischief, pretending to be serious. 'She told me herself she's sensational between the sheets. You're sure you don't fancy a fling with her?'

'No more than you fancy getting back with Hugh,' he said, and she couldn't work that out at once. When she stared he said, 'If you were sure you wouldn't be remembering what I said. Your doubts are your own.'

Why was Fergus stirring things still? Why had he taken such a dislike to Hugh? She challenged him. 'Why don't you like Hugh?'

'This isn't personal.' Both his voice and face were expressionless. 'This is a professional opinion. I wouldn't be much use as a journalist, interviewing all sorts, unless I was a competent judge of character, and I have a gut feeling that he has all the qualifications of a first-class shyster.' She gulped in air as he added, 'Successful so far,' before she could splutter,

'You said I was stupid, but you're the stupid one. That libel could get you sued for lottery-sized damages.'

He drawled, 'I doubt it. And you're only stupid where he's concerned. He's your blind spot. You've trusted him all your life, always taken his integrity for granted. Well, I don't think he knows the meaning of the word.'

This sickened her, so that she could hardly make herself look at him. Talk about two-faced. He could change in a flash from friend to enemy. One minute they were joking, the next he was spouting his malicious sleaze.

She said, 'You're nowhere near as good a journalist as you think you are, because your gut instinct couldn't be lousier. I have known Hugh all my life and he has only let me down once. Susan—'

'Forget Susan,' he said curtly. 'Bits on the side like Susan come cheap. More interesting is how he manages a lifestyle well above his means.'

'What are you on about? How would you know that?'

'I can find out most things if I put my mind to it.'

She was on her feet now. Their faces, hers furious, his unreadable, were only inches apart.

'Gutter press tactics,' she jeered.

'A little muck-raking can dredge up some surprising results.'

'So exactly what are you suggesting?'

'That Hugh Marshall has a young, inexperienced staff who wouldn't know half what he's up to.'

Except for Daisy. 'And what is that supposed to mean?'

'Call it creative accountancy.'

'*Embezzlement?* You're accusing Hugh of fiddling clients' funds because your gutter press reaction is that he might be?'

She had put all the scorn she could into that, but he said quietly, 'I've done some research and I wouldn't have him near any account of mine. Do you know how you stand with this trust fund of yours?'

'Of course I do.' She knew roughly what to expect next year from the fund her father had set up for her.

Hugh's firm had always acted as trustees, and the idea that her legacy might be at risk was preposterous.

She knew that, but Fergus's restless quest for news could have him setting Hugh up for in-depth investigation. Even with a firm as trustworthy as Marshall and Lindhurst muck-raking might stick.

She had to stop him before this went any further. She tried appealing. 'Please don't do this; it's horrible. My trust fund is none of your business, but Hugh *is* looking after it and I have every faith in him; he loves me.'

'I'm sure he does. You're a woman any red-blooded male could take to and you should be bringing him a sizeable sum.'

'God, you're disgustingly mercenary.' She could taste bitterness; this was revolting.

'I'm not, but I'd stake my life he is.' Fergus shook his head, puzzled. 'Did it never occur to you that the codicil might have had an influence on him?'

That made no sense. After a few seconds she said, 'Huh?'

'The codicil to your father's will.'

This was the first she had heard of a codicil, and Fergus was realising that. He said, 'You never saw the will?'

If she said again that it was none of his business he might shut up. She could ask her mother or Hugh what this was about. But Fergus knew and she needed to know.

She moved away from him to a window. Looking out, she started to shiver, as if she were out there in the cold and the darkness. She said, 'I was still at school and I'd gone on an expedition to Mozambique. For three weeks no one could get in touch with us;

we were studying tropical plants. We only went back
to the hotel in Maputo the day we were flying home.
My father was in hospital for an operation. Nothing
serious. He should have been well over it and home
again before I came home, but as it turned out it
couldn't have been more serious. They couldn't do
anything. They gave him a month to live and he lasted
two weeks. When I got off the plane Hugh and one
of our neighbours met me.'

She would always remember running to Hugh, looking for her parents, knowing at once that something
terrible had happened. And the drive from the airport,
with Hugh sombre and silent at the wheel, her
mother's friend with her arms around the girl whose
life had just fallen apart.

Clancy said now, 'It was all over. The funeral, everything. My mother had a sort of breakdown for a
while, but everybody was kind and Hugh and his father were always there for us. My father had made a
will much earlier, providing for my mother with a trust
fund for me.'

She paused. Fergus said nothing, waiting until she
said, 'Nobody told me about a codicil. You've seen
it? Why did you want to see my father's will?'

'It's got to be this minder business.' He grinned
wryly, as if his motive amused him. 'I took a dislike
to Hugh, I felt he was not to be trusted, and with you
banging on about how much you relied on him I wondered if that will had any loopholes that could be slithered through.'

'How did you get hold of the will?' As if it mattered. She was asking that to postpone the real question.

'Anyone can check on a probate register. Twenty-five pence a page, two pounds by post.'

'Easy as that?' She had to swallow before she could go on. 'And there was something added?'

'Witnessed five days before his death by James Marshall and Marguerite Davis.' Hugh's father and Daisy. 'If you and Hugh Marshall marry before you're twenty-five he gets half the final settlement.'

The words went off like a small explosion in her skull, leaving her ears ringing and her voice echoing, 'Is that legal? He was ill, dying.'

'But clear in his mind. He conducted business from his hospital bed. He knew what he was doing.'

Fergus knew more about her father's final days than she did. She had been still a schoolgirl and they had protected her, but she should have been advised on this. She demanded, 'Why did nobody tell me?' although it was useless asking him.

'Ask them,' he said.

She grabbed her coat and ran out into the night, turning an ankle on a cobblestone, slowing down but with her mind racing ahead. Her mother must know. Hugh and Daisy had to know. The shock had unhinged her emotionally, like learning you had been adopted, or were a twin whose sibling had died at birth. She ran upstairs into her mother's room, flushed and breathless, still carrying her coat. She hadn't paused to put it on.

Esta had been asleep, and when Clancy switched on the light she stirred, keeping her eyes closed and turning her head away. 'Mother.' Clancy gave her shoulder a shake. 'Wake up, I want to talk to you.'

'Now?' Esta's eyes opened a slit. 'Oh, Clancy. Can't it wait?'

Clancy leaned over her. 'It's waited long enough. You are awake? You are listening to me? I've just heard what my father added to his will before he died.'

'What?' Esta shrugged herself up from the sheets, still half asleep.

'The codicil. That if Hugh marries me before the balance of the fund is due he gets half. You'd have to know about that, wouldn't you? You did see the will, didn't you?'

'Yes, I saw it.' Her mother yawned. 'I was there when he signed it. Why are you bothering me about it at this time of the night?'

'Nobody told me,' Clancy snapped. 'The first I heard was ten minutes ago. Why wasn't I told?'

'Weren't you? I don't remember. I thought you were, but I never bothered about it. It was just something your father wanted to do when he knew he wouldn't be around to look after you. You were set on being a gardener, and at the time that didn't seem like much of a future to us. He knew how you felt about Hugh, and how Hugh felt about you.' She yawned again, then laughed a little. 'He knew you were never any good with money; he wanted Hugh to look after you.'

I was seventeen, Clancy could have reminded her, always overspending and coaxing hand-outs from her father...

'Anyhow,' said her mother, between the sheets again, 'I always knew you and Hugh were made for each other, and so did your father, so why are you making such a fuss? Hugh loves you.' Her eyes closed and she said drowsily, 'You can't imagine he's thinking of your money; he has far too much integrity to give that a thought.' And Clancy thought what a coincidence it was that her mother should have come up with that word too.

She passed a restless night. She couldn't believe that greed had influenced Hugh. He had always cared for her. She *was* making a fuss. But Fergus had this knack of disturbing her, and she would have preferred hearing about the codicil from anybody else.

He was too knowledgeable, was Fergus. He could find out most things he set his mind to. And in the still of the night she lay wondering what he might confront her with next.

Come morning she was listless, and given the chance she might have stayed in bed another hour or two. It was the weekend, she had no business appointments today, but for once her mother was down bright and early, calling up the stairs, 'Do you know what time it is?'

Clancy showered and dressed and put on some make-up and was sitting at the kitchen table two minutes ahead of Hugh arriving at the front door. When the bell rang and her mother said brightly, 'I'll get it,' and skipped into the hall Clancy could have put money on who was ringing the bell.

Hugh seated himself in the chair opposite Clancy and said, 'Now, what's all this about?' like a family doctor with a patient who had developed spots.

'Come off it,' she said ironically. 'She's rung you and briefed you so we all know what's up for discussion.'

Her mother was pouring Hugh a cup of coffee. He said, 'Thanks,' before he said to Clancy, 'The codicil. Good Lord, I never realised you didn't know about it, but I'd have hoped you know I'd never touch your money except in your interests. I want to marry you because you are the woman I want to spend my life with, but if it makes you happier we'll get married after your twenty-fifth birthday, when the codicil is null and void.'

Even Fergus couldn't sneer at that offer, and Clancy's mother clicked her tongue at Clancy. 'Well, I hope you're satisfied.'

Who wouldn't be?

Hugh took Clancy's hand then, holding it tight, looking into her eyes. 'I love you,' he said huskily. 'Your father had to know that; he was giving us his blessing, trusting you to me.'

Hugh's eyes were a light blue, like shallow water, and looking straight into them should have taken her breath away or at least kept her looking back. Fergus's dark eyes could reach into her mind, but she could turn away from Hugh as if there was no bond between them at all.

He hung onto her hand until she sat back in her chair, giving him the choice of letting go or sprawling across the table. He let her go with a twisted smile. 'You don't have to tell me who's been reading your father's will. That bloody journalist. Nor do you have to tell me why he's checking your finances,' Hugh went on. 'I can tell you that. He's on the make.'

Her lips twitched, but the harder she tried to get serious or indignant the funnier that became, and suddenly she was laughing out loud.

'Now don't get hysterical,' Hugh advised, like the family doctor again, and she wiped her eyes, her shoulders still shaking.

'Have another coffee when you've finished that one,' she said. 'I'm going along to the studio.'

He started to stand up. 'I'll go with you.'

'No, you won't,' she said, and left them, knowing her mother would sigh and sit down at the table and say how tiresome it was that Clancy should be fussing over something they had both forgotten because it didn't matter at all.

Her keys were still in her pocket, though she could easily have dropped them rushing home carrying her coat last night. She had not locked the studio door and she did now. She had left Fergus behind. His car must have been parked near; he would have left as soon as she did. She wasted no time getting her little van out of the garage and herself away from her mother and Hugh.

She expected one or both of them to come out of the house when they heard her engine start up, but if they did they were too late. She was onto the road, taking a quick turn-off while the road behind her was still clear, in case Hugh's car was following.

She had no plans for going anywhere. She could make business or social calls. She could drive into a town and shop and lunch, or just drive around listening to the radio or CDs. Or she could go to the mill house.

She cruised for a while, but before very long she found herself near the river on which the mill stood, and then she decided that she should tell Fergus that Hugh had no designs on her trust fund and there had been nothing sinister in her not having been told about the codicil.

The town's main streets were busy on a Saturday morning, and she took her van into the narrow lane that skirted the millpond. Compared with the river, the millpond had been a sluggish backwater, but today the surface was choppy, and near the wheel the water foamed, churning under the great rotating slats. Clancy nearly took her van off the towpath, goggling at it.

She hit the brakes, bringing the van to a juddering jolt, jumped out and ran to the bridge. The wheel was turning just as it should, slow and steady, and as Fergus came out of the house she waved from the bridge and carolled, 'It's a miracle.'

He joined her. 'Of course it is. Miracles happen all the time.'

'So how did you fix this one?'

'No problem,' he said.

She had known what had to be done and he had done it. Specialists had restored fitting and alignments and since earlier this morning this had become a working mill again. She was speechless, too thrilled for words. She watched the huge wheel going round with a pride and a pleasure that were almost painful. She flung her arms round him, telling him, 'This is the best surprise. This is a miracle—and they don't happen all the time. They're very rare, are miracles. Oh, I love it, I love—' She held back just in time.

'My pleasure,' he said, and she was sure he hadn't guessed what she had nearly told him.

But she stopped hugging and said, 'Honestly, I don't know what I'm doing.' She laughed. 'I'm all of a dither.'

'Coffee? Breakfast?' he suggested.

'Yes, please.' She might be hungry, and she wanted to go into the house through the dividing door to see the workings of the mill.

Half an hour later she was still too excited to do more with a plate of scrambled eggs than fork it around and swallow morsels.

Fergus said, 'Did you ask about the codicil?'

'It was nothing,' she said. 'Both of them seemed to think I knew, and Hugh said we'd get married after my birthday so it wouldn't apply.'

She could hear the creaking of the wheel and the splashing of water and it was almost like the rain and the river at the little hotel, the same feeling of being in a hide-out, warm and secure and cut off from the world outside.

'Very generous of him,' Fergus drawled.

'Well, it does prove he isn't swindling me.'

'Like hell it does.' He lounged on the sofa beside her and she put down her plate. The lovely lair-like atmosphere had gone; he was making her face her doubts again.

His words were slow and implacable. 'Hughie-boy is cheating you. He's conning you in every way.'

'I won't believe that.'

'Financially he's juggling accounts. And emotionally he's short-changing you. You say he loves you—well, I'll go along with that; you suit him. But he's got you believing he's your soulmate.'

She had always thought Hugh was, but Fergus was very close to her now. So close that she was resting against him and he was stroking her hair, one of his arms on the sofa behind her. This was pleasant. If she closed her eyes she could drift away.

Fergus said, 'You're off the cologne?'

'What?'

'The aftershave that used to addle your brain.'

'Not since I broke the bottle.'

'That's one problem less. What else makes you believe you were meant for each other?'

They were playing games, and she went along with it 'I've been hearing that for years.'

'Hearsay,' he said. 'Inadmissible evidence.'

'Evidence? What are you? The prosecuting attorney?'

'Just getting the facts.' He smiled down at her, lying in the crook of his arm. Even smiling his mouth was hard, and she wondered if he would kiss her and what would happen if he did.

'You're not going to fall apart again when he touches you?' he said. 'You *are* over that?'

Her starry-eyed confidence that Hugh's caresses were all the sexual satisfaction she could ever want had dimmed lately. She murmured, 'Uh-huh,' and left it at that, fiercely aware that Fergus's hand was brushing her cheek, quickening the nerves under her skin like an electric current, from her cheek to her jawbone, running down her spine, leaving her very bones tingling. Under layers of clothing she was being turned on, as if she was naked in the arms of her lover.

He could do that just by stroking her hair, brushing her cheek. If this went any further she would spin right out of control. Her body was arching to meet him. Holding back was so hard that her No was hardly more than a whisper.

He said, 'Why not?'

'This is a load of chemistry.' It might be entirely physical, but it was the first time Clancy had encountered a sensual power strong enough to scare her silly. Hugh had used to send her weak at the knees. Fergus could be turning her into one raging erogenous zone.

'That it is,' he said.

She managed to pull slightly out of his reach, protesting, 'I can't do this.'

He took her face in his hands and kissed her slowly, 'You can do it very well,' he told her. And she did.

She was brilliant. From the moment she kissed him back everything he did and she did followed naturally. Passion and pleasure came together, as though he knew every inch of her, and she reached instinctively, sometimes receptive, sometimes voracious. It was easy loving, rising to a peak of ecstasy from which she was flying light years higher than she had ever known before, and she floated down slowly and gently, feeling safe and happy all the way.

Around midday they set out to walk to the local for lunch, although Clancy could hardly bear to leave the mill. She could have watched the wheel turning for hours. The water under the bridge flowed fast from the impetus of the wheel, reminding her of the flooding river and another bridge. She said suddenly, 'Do you think I'll panic when I go swimming again? I really thought I was drowning. I'd hate to find I've developed a phobia.'

He said, 'Next time you give yourself some time off I'll take you to a pool I found, in a jungle near the ruins of an ancient temple. The water is as green as your eyes and you can walk into it over the white stones or dive where it's deep.'

She could imagine the scene, in brilliant colours, like something out of a TV travelogue or a glossy brochure. Too perfect to be true. Although there might be another little miracle. A fabulous journey that might just happen. She said, 'Twenty-four hours' notice and I'll be packed and ready.'

They walked down the high street with Bruno at their heels to the black and white inn with the thatched roof. This picture-postcard Tudor building was fully booked by tourists for most of the year but now, early December, a vacancies board hung from the inn sign.

Inside, about a third of the tables were occupied with lunchtime customers, and Clancy and Fergus settled themselves in a corner. 'Well-behaved dogs welcomed', said a notice, and Bruno lay under the table looking well behaved.

Sara, the young woman who ran the hotel with her husband, was an old school friend of Clancy's. She had seen Fergus during the week, and she came smiling from behind the bar to inform them, 'I think she's still in her room. Shall I tell her you're here?'

'Who?' Clancy asked.

'Your fiancée,' Sara said to Fergus, her smile fading when she saw how her announcement was being received.

The girl occupying one of their best bedrooms had booked in last night and been perfectly sweet, telling Sara that her fiancé was Fergus McKenzie, who was staying at the mill house. She had insisted on giving him some privacy to get on with some very important writing he was doing, and friends had recommended this inn to her. She had talked a lot about the man she was going to marry, flashing a three-stone diamond engagement ring.

Now Clancy was shaking her head, and the man called McKenzie said, 'Please ask her to join us.' He was stunning, no wonder the girl had raved about him, but now he was grim-faced, and Sara decided he was not one she herself would care to cross. She hoped Clancy knew what she was doing here.

While they waited Clancy said, 'It is Angela, of course.'

'How many madwomen do you think I've lined up?'

'Is she mad?'

'Mad on getting her own way. She and Hughie-boy have a lot in common. But this has got to stop right now. Will you back me up?'

'Sure,' Clancy said automatically, as Angela came into the dining room and stood looking around, spotting them and almost running towards them. Out of that coat she was as thin as an anorexic.

She turned a few heads. Not least because she was rushing with her arms wide, set on embracing somebody. Fergus got up and clamped her arms down to her sides. Then he reached for another chair, drawing it to their table. He said, 'Cut out the play-acting. Sit down and don't make another move.'

She pulled a laughing face. 'I knew you'd come. If I stayed here I knew you'd find me.'

He said, 'I haven't found you because I wasn't looking for you.' Other occupied tables were out of earshot of low voices, and Fergus spoke quietly and grimly. 'Any support I've given you was for Alan's sake. His memory is the only bond between us. But you've told Clancy we're lovers and the landlady here believes we're heading for marriage. A pack of lies, as you damn well know. So in future keep out of my way, and remember I was Alan's colleague and Alan's friend, and as far as you are concerned that was all I ever was.'

When he paused Angela waited, head on one side, as if there might be more. Then she said, 'You don't mean that.'

Fergus exchanged a wry glance with Clancy. Then he said to Angela, 'When you were with Alan I always thought you were a selfish little bitch. I never fancied you then, nor do I now. But if you can't get that into your head meet Clancy again, because she is the woman I am going to marry.'

CHAPTER EIGHT

'WHY did you *say* that?' Clancy gasped, walking quickly along the pavement and away from the hotel.

Fergus kept up with her in spite of his limp. 'I needed something drastic enough to stop her putting an announcement in the press and getting the banns read.'

Clancy shot him a sidewards glare, checking if he was smiling, because she was not amused, and snapping, 'Well, you've put me right on the spot.'

'Sorry about that. I should have taken her seriously before now.'

Angela was obviously not the girl to take a hint, and saying he was marrying Clancy should prove to her that Fergus was not available. It was not the truth, of course. It was a crazy thing to have said and there would be plenty of misunderstanding before that rumour was scotched.

'So we're engaged, are we?' she said testily.

'It can be a very brief engagement.' He sounded serious, conciliatory, but then he did grin. 'Anyway you owe me. For getting Hugh off your back. You can do the same for me with Angela.'

There might have been fireworks at the hotel if they had stayed around. Angela had asked Clancy, 'Is this true?' and Clancy had nodded dumbly. What else could she have done?

Then Clancy had said to Fergus, 'I'd like to leave now,' and beaten a fast retreat. Fergus had followed her and Bruno, taking off from under the table, had nearly sent a large lady spinning.

Clancy had led the way down the high street and she was still striding between the pedestrians on the pavement. Lord knows what Angela was telling Sara, what anyone else in the dining room who knew Clancy would be thinking. As for her mother and Hugh, if this news reached them before she did it would be volcano eruption time.

She had to assure them it was a charade, a sham to stop some woman believing that Fergus was in love with her. Angela would take some explaining, that was for sure. They were eager for any sleaze about Fergus, and this poor woman claiming she had been passionately led on and ruthlessly let down would suit them fine.

When they reached the mill Clancy said, 'Consider yourself paid in full for the wheel.'

'A fair deal,' said Fergus.

'So much for lunch,' she said.

He went to the fridge and took out two cans of lager, holding them up. She nodded and he pulled the ringed tab on one, handing it to her. As she poured it into a glass he opened the second.

Her throat was dry. She gulped a little of the ice-cold liquid and he took hold of her hand. 'With this ring,' he said. The ring just went over her knuckle, the metal tab still attached, looking ridiculous, summing up a zany situation.

She simpered, 'I didn't know you cared. This is so sudden. I'm at a loss for words.'

'That's a first,' he said.

'No, it isn't.' The tab-ring was not coming off as easily as it had gone on and she began tugging at it.

'I didn't know what to say when you told her that, and if my mother and Hugh get to hear about it I don't know how I'm going to persuade them that you haven't been beastly to dear little Angela.'

He said fervently, 'I wish I had. My mistake was when I was sorting out Alan's affairs. She was distraught—genuinely, I think—and I said, "Anything you need, anything at all." I should have hedged that.'

'You did say *anything*. The lady took you at your word.' She began to giggle, and he was laughing with her, until her giggles became great whoops of laughter, both of them laughing their heads off so that Bruno's ears pricked up and Clancy's eyes began to water. This was hysterical stuff. Her with a ring off a lager tin stuck on her finger, after a public announcement that Fergus intended to marry her, and Angela the 'raving fantasist' left with an enthralled audience who had popped into the hotel for lunch.

Clancy waved her ringed finger. 'If I can't get this off it will be the final proof I'm in cuckoo land.'

Her mobile rang on the table and that stopped her laughter, although her 'Hello' came through twitching lips.

'Clancy. Sara here. What's going on?' Sara sounded quite unlike her usually bouncy self. '*Are* you marrying him?'

Clancy evaded a straight answer. 'We have—a sort of understanding.' And nearly got the giggles again at Fergus's approving nod.

'This woman…' Sara said. 'I heard what he said about marrying you; he said it quite loudly, didn't he? And she saw I'd heard, and when you both walked out she beckoned me over. She was still sitting at the table and she asked me if I was a friend of yours. Well,

I said I was, of course and she said, ''Tell her to take very good care.''' Sara drew a long breath. 'And she said ''Tell her she should be afraid.'''

Clancy had expected Angela to create a scene which could have been more embarrassing than these hammy threats. She asked, 'What did she do then?'

'Went up to her room.'

'That was all?'

'It was all she said.' Sara was struggling to get across something beyond the words. 'But it was the way she looked, sitting there, playing with a steak knife she'd picked up from the table as if she was testing it for sharpness. And her eyes. You know me, I don't go round imagining things, but her eyes were *murderous*. I got the chills just looking at her.'

Sara was giving Clancy an uneasy shiver. She said, 'Thanks, and I will take care. She lost her partner not very long ago. I'll tell you all about it some time.'

'Right,' said Sara, ending with a final warning, 'She's a weirdo. She was sweet as sugar yesterday, but today she's the wicked witch. If you hadn't got out I think she could have used that knife; she's really dangerous.'

When she'd switched off the phone Clancy asked Fergus, 'Is Angela dangerous? She told Sara to tell me I should be very afraid, while she was sitting at the table playing with a sharp knife. And with murder in her eyes, according to Sara.'

Fergus didn't seem surprised. 'She trained as an actress. Alan got her a few small parts on TV, and she had been with a touring company. This was probably a line out of one of the melodramas.'

'She impressed Sara.'

'Sara didn't know she was dealing with a drama

queen.' Clancy hoped that Angela *was* all words, because, like Sara, she found the wicked witch playing with a steak knife rather alarming.

Clancy was fiddling with the lager ring again, and spent the next few minutes holding her hand under the cold water tap and smearing on soap before she could ease it off. As she stroked her puffy finger her phone rang again.

Fergus said, 'Shall I—?'

'I'll take it.' The calls would go on until she switched off, but she took this call and it was the caller she wanted least. Her mother, screaming at her. One of the lunching ladies had wasted no time, and Esta Lindhurst was screeching that she couldn't believe it, that Clancy was mad. Where was she now? She must come home immediately.

Fergus took the phone from her and cut off the call. 'We should be explaining to her,' he said.

She knew she should be explaining, but her mother sounded in no state to listen and Clancy was in no hurry to be screamed at. 'I'm not going home to that just yet,' she decided.

She needed some self-control herself before she could explain the situation, and the rest of the day, which they spent in the countryside, restored her confidence and calmed her nerves. They came back to the mill for her to collect her van after a leisurely evening meal at a restaurant that was new to Clancy but had proved quite a find.

'Coffee?' Fergus suggested.

She thought not. In the mill house she could lose all sense of time in a wonderfully satisfying way, and it was such a temptation, but she should be putting things right with her mother. She had decided what she was going to say as soon as they came face to face. I am not marrying Fergus, nor does he want to marry me. He said that to shut up a woman who's been a nuisance for months. He and I are friends, but there is no question of marriage whatever you've been hearing.

Beyond that she would rather not go tonight. It was getting late, and if her mother insisted on more details that would be easier for both of them after a night's rest.

Her mother was waiting for her. There were lights on but at first, coming into the hall, Clancy thought she might be in bed, it was so quiet down here.

She was in the drawing room, in her usual chair, and Clancy started to speak in the doorway. 'I am—'

'I don't want to hear it.' Esta bit off her own words, overriding Clancy's. 'Do you have any idea? Any idea what you are doing? Making a fool of Hugh. And of me. All my friends are sorry for me, the way you're carrying on. But of course my feelings don't matter, do they? They never did; you never listened to me. You must be enjoying yourself, causing all this trouble. And for what? Some man you picked up, or who picked you up. And he is no good for you, no good for any woman. Anyone can see that. So now you listen. You either stop this or you are no longer welcome here.'

The tirade rained down on Clancy like a storm of stinging hailstones. She stood there, shaking her head, trying to protest, until the last words—which were unbelievable. She stammered, 'What? *What?*'

Her mother didn't meet Clancy's eyes, and a slow flush was suffusing her face, but she said, 'Your home, your family—or him.'

This house had always been Clancy's home; she couldn't imagine its doors being locked against her. But there was a lump in her throat that stopped her saying, Please don't do this to me.

Tomorrow she would, because this was absurd, but right now perhaps she should leave her mother alone. If she went up to her room her mother would follow, so she had to get out of the house. She said quietly, 'All right, I'm going.'

'Go on then, get *out*,' her mother hissed.

Clancy had a home of her own. She owned the mill house. She could stay there for the night. She drove through the dark empty streets, shocked and bewildered because she had never expected this. It made her think of the Tarot card of the falling tower, a fortress that was no longer a safe place. Better not to dwell on that when it was the second card that had made her blood run cold.

She heard Bruno barking as her van drew up, and Fergus opened the house door before she could climb out of her seat behind the wheel. Almost at once her smile was making her face ache, but she kept smiling when he reached her and she said, 'I've been chucked out.'

'*What?*'

'My mother has disowned me. The option is either you or them. If it's you I'm never to darken her door again.'

He put an arm around her, guiding her towards the house, 'They're hot on blackmail,' he said. 'This is the second time they've tried this tactic.'

Hugh, after the night at the club. She said, 'But Hugh apologised; he'd just lost his temper. *She'd* been thinking about it. She had it off pat. She wouldn't let me get a word in. She said she didn't want to hear.'

'Shall I go back with you and we'll make her listen?'

Not tonight. It would have taken very little more tonight to have had Clancy in tears. She felt like a lost child, wailing, 'What could we say to her? All she wants to hear is that I'm back with Hugh, which is where I belong.'

'Then she's out of luck,' he said briskly. 'She shouldn't have a hope in hell of ever hearing you say that.'

Her mother had hurt her bitterly, but she had someone to turn to. A man who was strong and intuitive enough to stop her feeling too sorry for herself. Bruno was welcoming her, his tail swishing happily. The dog settled on the rug at her feet as she sank onto the sofa.

Fergus was standing, looking down at her, and she knew that if she burst into tears he would wipe the tears away, and that his touch would be all the solace she needed. She held back the tears, blinking a couple of times, and he said gently, 'She'll come round. She's frightened. She thought Hugh Marshall meant security for you, and I'm the joker in the pack.'

'She thinks you're no good.' That was hilarious when Fergus was the best thing that had ever happened to Clancy, and she mimicked her mother's waspish words. '"No good for me, no good for any woman. Anyone can see that."'

He did his devilish leer. 'Maybe she's not as daft as I thought.'

He sat down beside her and took her in his arms, stroking her hair and planning tomorrow, which he thought they might spend with friends of his. She would look forward to that. She would like to meet his friends and get away from here for a few more hours.

Her mother's rejection was losing some of its sting. It was sad and hurtful, but as Fergus said, she must come round in the end, and accept that Clancy would always look on Hugh as one of her dearest friends, but that the prospect of a lifetime with him was out of the question.

Clancy would rather spend a lifetime alone. She was happy enough now—although she was hardly alone—curled up against Fergus, beginning to feel she knew the couple he was telling her about. He was a TV producer; she was a cookery writer. They lived on a longboat and they had been together for years.

That was the way it ought to be. With the right one. As Fergus was right for Clancy. And realising that made her heart start hammering, playing havoc with her breathing. She had always found him attractive, liked him enormously, even possessively. She had told herself theirs was a rapport that would be a thrilling memory in her busy and happy life when he went away. But she knew now that without him she would spend a lifetime in a cold and lonely world where she would never be truly happy.

This was not how he felt about her. There was a possibility that he never would, and she would be mad to force the issue. I love you. Do you love me? That would have him telling her again that she was too good for Hugh but sure to meet someone else. Not him. He would make out a very good case as to why she should not be committing herself to him, while the only real reasons were that he did not love her that way and he certainly did not want commitment.

But she wanted him on any terms, and she would do nothing to jeopardise her chances. As Angela said—although this was not at all what Angela had had in mind—Clancy would be very careful. Not to show her feelings, and never to be demanding.

It would have been easy now to let the comforting closeness lead to the kind of caresses that would flare into mind-blowing passion where she would neither know nor care what she was babbling. Like, Don't ever leave me. Or, I love you, I love you, I love you.

She drew back a little, and he made no move to hold her. They might both be living in the mill house for a while but he needed space and privacy, not an intimate togetherness, and it was talk not lovemaking that went on between them until well past midnight when she said, 'I don't even have a toothbrush. I'll have to go back to collect some of my things.'

'Your mother might have had second thoughts.'

'Not yet.' Not after the way she had hissed, 'Go on, get out,' only a few hours before. Clancy had made her choice, but the ordeal had taken its toll and she felt a tide of fatigue sweep over her.

Fergus stood up. 'You take the sofa. I'll doss down upstairs.'

She was relieved he was not taking it for granted they would be sharing a bed. Suppose she talked in her sleep? Tonight she was fragile; tomorrow they might make other arrangements. She asked, 'Are you sure?'

'It's your pad.'

He gave her a shirt, and she remembered donning a shirt of his at the Fisherman's Rest, when she'd been delirious with a fever and running from the memory of Hugh and Susan. That all seemed a long time ago—

so much had happened since then. She had changed in so many ways.

Almost at once she was lulled into a deep and dreamless sleep.

When Fergus touched her cheek she opened her eyes and smiled. He was shaved, dressed, holding a mug of coffee. He must have been moving around in the bathroom and at the stove but she hadn't heard a thing. She was only awake now because he had woken her. She was still deliciously drowsy, and she took the coffee gratefully.

He said, 'We're going to buy some newspapers and get a toothbrush for you. Anything you fancy for breakfast?'

She wriggled happily. 'Lovely. Room service. Fruit?'

This *was* lovely. She drank a little coffee, then took the mug into the bathroom. She had been wearing jeans and a sweater yesterday. Unless she could get a change from home that was what she would be in today, and with no make-up, except the lipstick in her purse she would be looking pale and not very interesting when she met Fergus's friends.

She drank more coffee, then showered, and was drying herself on a big bath towel when she heard him back again in the main room. She only put a head and a hand round the door to get the toothbrush, and when she saw who was there she would have jumped back and shut the door. But Hugh had seen her.

So she came out, barefooted, well covered by the towel, acting unflapped—just mildly curious. 'Where is he?' Hugh demanded.

'Buying me a toothbrush,' she said.

Hugh looked at her and at the unmade bed as if the

sight of both was shattering, 'You're not just paying
me out for Susan, are you? Not all this?'

'Of course not.'

'Oh, Clancy.' His voice shook. 'You're infatuated.
You think he saved your life; you think he'll always
be here for you. You're so naive, you always were.
Your father knew that. That's why he wanted me to
take care of you.'

'I was hardly more than a child when my father
died,' she reminded him.

'You're acting like a child now,' Hugh countered.

With Hugh she had remained a dreaming teenager.
With Fergus she was all woman, incredibly and passionately alive.

'Won't you come back home with me?' Hugh's
voice was soft and cajoling. 'Your mother is distraught.' Hugh would know about that, Clancy
thought. They had very likely planned this latest
blackmail together.

Her answer was a flat, 'No.'

She was clutching her bathtowel, Hugh was moving
closer, and she had to decide whether she should risk
holding him off verbally or if she should dash for the
bathroom and lock the door. He could be right about
her ending up alone, but she would never need Hugh
again.

Bruno came in first, spotting Hugh and beginning
to growl. At a word from Fergus the growling stopped,
but the dog stayed wary and watchful. 'Glad I caught
you,' said Fergus. 'I saw your car through the news-
agent's window.'

He must have come back at a fast stride. Clancy
could probably have handled Hugh, but she was not
dressed for a scuffle and she was glad to see Fergus.

His arrival stopped Hugh taking another step towards her.

'I'll be going,' Hugh said, looking at Clancy. 'But remember that I love you. I'd do anything in the world for you.'

Fergus drawled, 'You've already done more than enough for Clancy.'

The two men were facing each other. Hugh's face was flushed and she saw a vein throbbing in his temple. Fergus had that mask-like stillness. It seemed to Clancy that the atmosphere was as heavy as the air before a thunderstorm, then Hugh turned away.

The door was open. When he reached it he said, 'You've got the wheel working. It's even worse with that noise in your ears; I always said this place was unhealthy.'

But he took the heaviness with him. When he had gone Clancy breathed freely. Hugh could not have sounded more understanding, but when pleading had failed to move her he would have tried the sexual technique that had rarely failed him in the past. It could have been quite awful if Fergus had not come back.

Fergus asked, 'What did he have to say?'

'He thinks I'm living and sleeping with you, but he's ready to overlook everything if I'll go back to him.'

'A very generous gesture.' Fergus's praise was wildly exaggerated. 'And he's still a con-merchant. Get some clothes on and I'll take you to meet some genuine folk.'

Clancy had a stroke of luck on the way to her day out. When she let herself in her mother was not at home, so she was spared another painful scene. She had left Fergus in the car outside. She had joked about keeping the engine running for a quick getaway and been very definite about not wanting him going in with her.

In her bedroom she packed a case with clothes that should serve her for the week, putting in make-up and toiletries, wasting no time. She had the case at the top of the stairs when he came into the hall and called up to her, 'Everything all right?'

'There's nobody here.'

He came up the stairs to take the case and she went back to gather an armful of bedding. She had bought it. She had paid for all manner of things. But she was only taking what she needed urgently. She left a note on the kitchen table. 'I've taken some of my things. I do want to talk to you, although it is over between Hugh and me. I love you.'

In the car she applied enough make-up to put a glow on her face, then settled back to enjoy the ride and the company. Fergus was an ideal companion for a long-ish journey. Serious and informative when they listened to the radio news, witty and wicked when they were cruising along, talking and joking.

The miles slid by and the time passed almost too quickly before they were approaching the stretch of the River Thames where the longboat was moored. Clancy wanted to meet Fergus's friends, but she would have been quite content to drive on, just the two of them, stopping for nobody.

All the same, Dinah and Dan Horobin were worth getting to know. Fergus parked the car on the towpath and he and Clancy and the dog walked across a narrow bridge toward an islet. Before they reached it a man was on the deck of a boat, booming a greeting. The welcome was for Fergus, of course. He was the guest they were waiting for. Bruno seemed to be a favourite, and because Clancy was with Fergus she was accepted whole-heartedly.

Outside it was a grey winter's day, but inside the boat was warm and bright, with red curtains at the windows, mellow wood panelling and old-fashioned oil lamps adapted for electricity. And one of the best-equipped kitchens Clancy had ever seen.

Dan, who was middle-aged, middle height, slightly overweight but with a thin, clever face, commuted to wherever his work took him. The galley was Dinah's workroom. On a shelf among classic cookery books were half a dozen with Dinah's name.

She was wearing a loose black shirt and black jeans, grey hair springing back from a smiling unlined face. A table was laid for four, and while Dan and Fergus were discussing the script Fergus was writing Clancy sat on a stool in the galley section and watched Dinah adding a large tub of crème fraîche and four table-spoons of mango chutney to a gently simmering curry.

The women were on the same wavelength. A dedicated cook and a creative gardener had plenty in common. Clancy found Dinah easy to talk to and listen to, and as they sat around the table, half an hour or so later, she felt that she was among friends.

The talk came round to Angela. They had heard she had Fergus's address at the mill house and they both considered her a nuisance and a bit of a joke. Dinah asked Clancy, 'Have you met her?'

'Yes.'

'Well, don't believe a word she says. She's not a bad actress and she can put on quite an act.'

'I've gathered that,' Clancy said, and Dan chuckled.

'She's psychic as well. She gets—you know—the vibes, and she's dynamite at the palm-reading.'

'Time you put a stop to her nonsense.' Dinah was being practical and firm with Fergus. 'Nobody could have done more to help her after Alan went, but she's got to realise that it can't go on.'

Fergus said, 'I couldn't agree more,' and Dinah beamed at him and then at Clancy.

When the shadows of night were falling they left, with a box of exotic jams and pickles and a marrow-bone in a plastic bag for Bruno. Dinah's farewell words were, 'Lovely to have met you, Clancy. Take care of that leg, Fergus, and for goodness' sake do something about Angela.'

Dan's words were, 'And get a move on with the script.'

Sometimes Clancy must have taken Fergus away from his laptop, and she was having conscience pangs about that. But for the next week he should be able to get on with his work—and she should be concentrating on hers.

'They liked you,' said Fergus as she snuggled down in her seat.

She said, 'I hope so. I liked them very much.'

They had really made her welcome. It had been a comfortable kind of day, and because she had drunk several glasses of a pleasantly robust red, while Fergus, who was driving, had stayed with non-alcoholic, before long she could hardly keep her eyes open. And within a few minutes of her eyes closing she was asleep.

She was still yawning while they unpacked the car and she started taking clothes out of her case. They had left the sofa down here as a bed, and when Fergus said goodnight and he and Bruno went upstairs she didn't try to delay him. She was tired, and he had to be. She had to be up early in the morning and he must want to get on with the script his friend was hassling him for.

She put out tomorrow's clothes and shot in and out of the bathroom. The lullaby of the river and having Fergus within call relaxed and comforted her, so that instead of lying awake thinking about her problems she was asleep again almost as soon as her head hit the pillow.

Next morning she drank coffee and ate a round of toast, moving around the room while Fergus sat at the table, coffee mug at his elbow, going over papers. 'See you this evening,' she said, hovering, frightened at how much she wanted him to kiss her.

He didn't. He looked up from the keyboard, smiled, and said, 'I'll be here.'

As she got into her van she supposed she had had a narrow escape. If he had kissed her goodbye she might have clung on that moment longer that would have given her away.

She had a busy schedule, with no time for day-dreaming, although knowing she was going home to Fergus after work would be more than enough to keep her cheerful. She parked the van in the drive of her mother's house and made herself walk, not run, round the side of the house and across the lawns. In future she might use the gate from a side road that led into the garden that had been a field. That way she need not go near her old home and there would be no risk of anyone stopping and harassing her.

Her mind was on her plans for today. Christmas was coming, and a man wanted his patio given a festive touch as a surprise for his wife. Nothing too elaborate or expensive. It would be a fun theme rather than a professional project. The couple were friends of Clancy's and she was doing this as a favour, only charging expenses. This morning she was collecting some bargain statuary. This afternoon she would be back at the drawing board. She reached the little clearing where her studio stood believing that nothing could spoil her day.

What's that doing there? was her first thought when she saw the floral ring on the doorstep. White flowers were conspicuous with the dark trees around and the overcast skies, but as she walked towards it she saw that the lilies were drooping, the petals of the carnations and gypsophila were turning yellow. The flowers were dying. It was a funeral wreath. A black-edged card had been cut so that all that remained were the printed words 'With Deepest Sympathy'.

'Bloody Angela,' Clancy said aloud. This was just her sort of melodramatic gesture. She must have taken it from a churchyard skip and that chilled Clancy. Imagining Angela rooting among the decaying tributes, searching for a card from which she could remove the personal message, finding where Clancy's studio was and creeping in here yesterday or during the night.

Picking it up made Clancy feel as though a poisonous odour was rising from it, and even after she had binned it she was still nauseous.

She almost rang Fergus, but she stopped on the third digit when Bets arrived, so white-faced that her freckles stood out like a disfiguring rash. 'Come and see,' Bets almost sobbed. 'Come and see what they've done. Somebody's done this, haven't they?'

Somebody had wielded weedkiller in withering patches along the pathway from the side gate that Bets took coming in to work. The damage was limited, the plants and undergrowth could be replaced, but Bets loved coming here, loved her job, and this had upset her almost as badly as if a gang of thugs had wrecked her home.

Clancy was furious. Not with the sickness that the withered wreath had caused, but hot with rage. This was insufferable vandalism, and heaven knew what the idiot woman would be up to next.

'Shall I ring the police?' Bets asked, and Clancy shook her head.

'I'll handle it. Make yourself a cup of tea; I won't be long.'

She rang Sara as soon as she had the van well away from the house and had drawn up by the side of the road, to find out if Angela was still at Sara's hotel.

She was. She had paid for a fortnight in advance and had caused no trouble since her performance with the steak knife. Did Clancy think she was dangerous?

Clancy said, 'She's an actress; she specialises in melodrama. She isn't dangerous but she is being a pain, and I'm on my way for some straight talking with her.'

Sara was looking out for Clancy. She came out of the kitchens at the back of the hotel as Clancy parked her van in the hotel car park, and told her, 'She's still in her room. I took her breakfast tray up a few minutes ago.'

Clancy rapped on the door and opened it as Angela called, 'Come in.'

She was sitting up in bed. Her shining hair was loose, and even without any make-up her face was almost flawless. She was eating a finger of toast, and when she saw Clancy she popped the last piece into her mouth and smiled as if she were savouring something delicious.

Clancy knew what that was. She put her hands on her hips and said, 'Any more and I'll sue you.'

'Any more of what?' Angela was all injured innocence. 'What am I supposed to have done?'

Of course she knew, but Clancy said, 'How about a withered wreath on my doorstep and weedkiller on my garden?'

Angela gave an actress's show of shock-horror, then she said, 'That sounds like a very dissatisfied customer.'

Clancy did not have unhappy clients. She worked with them until they were happy. 'Nothing to do with me.' Angela picked up another finger of toast. 'What does Fergus think about it?' Her eyes were bright and eager, as if this was something she had to know.

'I haven't told him,' said Clancy.

'But you will?' Angela was not acting now. She was holding her breath. And Clancy could see how much she wanted him told. That moment gave Clancy a sudden insight into the workings of Angela's mind. She was like a child playing spiteful tricks.

She wanted Clancy making a fuss, running to Fergus over what had been little more than aggravation so far. Angela would deny any involvement, of course, but surely her plan was to goad Clancy into a state of jitters where Fergus would lose patience with her as he had obviously lost patience with Angela. Only this time Angela would be the unflappable one and his latest love would be the burden.

Clancy said, 'I shan't bother Fergus. He's busy, and

I'm quite capable of dealing with ill-will, especially when I know where it's coming from. We were with Dan and Dinah Horobin yesterday and they warned me about you.'

The sharpness drained out of Angela's face, replaced by a blank look. In a sing-song voice she said, 'Why should I want to hurt you? I don't hate you. I'm sorry for you. You have no future with Fergus. No future at all. Your aura is black. Around you there is only darkness.'

'Oh, grow up,' Clancy snapped.

Sara was waiting in the corridor outside, and Clancy must have looked slightly shocked because Sara asked anxiously, 'Are you all right?'

Clancy said, 'You're right; she's a weirdo. It's the wicked witch again this morning. She's got it in for me but there's not much she can do. Just give me a ring, will you, if you catch her sticking pins into a doll?'

Sara was not at all sure this was funny. Having accepted a booking it would not be easy telling a customer to leave, but Sara was far from happy with weirdos in her hotel.

When Clancy got back to the studio Bets was on her second cup of coffee, still fuming over the weed-killer and waiting to hear where Clancy had been. Bets could not see the funny side either as Clancy tried to explain the situation without panicking her.

Clancy said, 'There's a woman who might try to cause some trouble for me, so double-check orders and phone calls and tell me if anything seems odd to you. She's harmless, but she's a pest!'

Bets's eyes were getting wider. 'Why's she doing this?'

Clancy grimaced. 'Because she doesn't like me being with the man I'm with.'

It didn't surprise Bets that some woman was jealous of Clancy, but weedkiller was a dirty trick. Bets said, 'You want to get a good lawyer on her.' As soon as she spoke she remembered that Hugh Marshall was a lawyer, but he was no longer the man with Clancy, and she blushed hotly.

Clancy said, 'We know one lawyer who wouldn't take the job,' and that got a grin out of Bets.

Clancy had had to warn Bets, who sometimes dealt with business matters, but she was not making a big production of this. If Angela did anything outrageous Fergus would have to be told, but Clancy felt she could handle a spoilt brat playing childish tricks.

The garden statuary had arrived in a builder's yard after some demolition work. There were no marble antique pieces but several weathered concrete figures, and Clancy got two rabbits and a small boy with pointed ears sitting cross-legged and playing a flute for the price of a cinema ticket.

They were loaded into her van and she delivered them to the house with the patio. Then it was back to her studio, parking in the road and walking past the scorched patches where Angela had directed the weedkiller like a blowtorch. If she had bought that locally it could be enough to give her game away. She was not too bright but she was a problem, and Clancy hoped there were no more surprises waiting for her.

There was one, but it had nothing to do with Angela and it should have pleased Clancy. As Clancy walked in Bets said, 'Your mother was here; she left you this.'

Esta had left a note in a sealed envelope: 'Please come home. Love you, Mother.' And that had to be a relief because Clancy truly wanted a reconciliation. But she did not want to go home—not to live there. She had begun to take it for granted that she would be living in the mill house as long as Fergus stayed, working apart most days but together for all the nights. She was pleased, of course, that her mother was no longer bitter, but she found herself wishing that Esta had waited a few more days, or even a few weeks, before asking her to come home.

She was in the office for the rest of the day, and when she was through she drove over to the mill house. She would decide tomorrow what to do about her mother's note. This evening she and Fergus would have a quiet meal together, and afterwards they might share the sofa bed. Coming home meant the mill house, because he was there and she was longing to see him.

He was where she had left him, at the table with the laptop, still immersed in his work, although he looked up and leaned back when she walked in. 'Strewth,' he said. 'Is it that time?'

She had hoped he might be as anxious to see her as she was to see him, but that was not how it was. She felt that she could have been later and he would have carried on working, maybe till bedtime, when he would have assumed she was staying some other place. He would hardly have noticed her absence while she had been counting the hours until they were together again.

'Have a good day?' he said.

'My mother left me a note.'

She took it out of her purse and gave it to him, with a silent prayer that he would say, 'Don't go.' But he said, 'This is a peace offering. You can go home.'

He was making no move to stop her leaving. He was working to a deadline, and, with the best will in the world, she had to be a disturbance. So it was, Go away, Clancy; she mustn't even think of saying, I want to stay with you, I want to be wherever you are... Because that would be making a nuisance of herself, playing Angela's game.

She said, 'I suppose I should hear what she has to say this time.'

He smiled and gave her back the note, and promised her. 'It will be, Welcome home.'

Esta opened the door before Clancy could get her key in the lock. She didn't do that often, nor did she usually stand at a loss for words as the wind blew gusts of cold air at them, before she managed to say, 'Come on in; it's freezing.'

But from then on Esta hid any embarrassment she might have felt. She chattered about having lunch with a friend, asked what Clancy had been doing today and put a frozen dinner in the microwave oven before she said huskily, 'What I said on Saturday—I'm sorry I upset you. I was upset myself. I was hasty.'

Clancy said, 'It's all right, so long as you understand that I can't marry Hugh.' She could no longer assure her mother that Fergus was only a friend when love surged through her like a current whenever she said his name.

But Esta did not want to talk about Fergus McKenzie. Almost as soon as the door had closed after Clancy on Saturday night she had realised that her outburst could have sent her daughter right into the arms of that man. When she had phoned Hugh he had said they had to be patient. Clancy was infatuated and infatuations did not last. This one would run its course until Clancy came to her senses, and the less fuss the better. Meanwhile there must be no more screaming matches. So Esta smiled sweetly now and said, 'Darling, of course I understand. I only want you to be happy.'

Clancy ate some of the microwaved cottage pie while her mother prattled on as if neither of them had a care in the world. Just like old times—as Clancy told Fergus, phoning him later from her bedroom. 'We're not talking about Hugh, and we are definitely not talking about you. But there's a lot of sweetness and light about and a strong whiff of hypocrisy.'

Fergus laughed. She heard the dog bark and wanted to be there so badly that it was like homesickness, as if she was phoning from a hotel room in a foreign land. 'Shall I see you tomorrow?' she asked. 'Shall I come to the mill after work, or are you too busy? By the way, how's the work going?'

'Pretty well, I think, and of course I want to see you.'

She would have gone round even if he had been busy. Without an invitation she might have limited her time, but she would have looked in to say hello. Now she said, 'Goodnight. Give Bruno a biscuit for me.'

Fergus said, 'Sleep well,' but she had a restless night. She missed the sounds of the mill wheel turning and she missed knowing that Fergus was near enough to hear if she called.

The following days that week were something of a charade. Most of Clancy's friends had been told what Fergus had said about marrying Clancy, but few of them took it seriously. Hugh shrugged it off. As far as he was concerned he and Clancy had a salvageable relationship. When she was at home with Clancy her mother never mentioned Fergus or Hugh, chattering away about anything else, and Clancy went into work early and spent the evenings with Fergus.

Not the nights. At night she slept in the bedroom she had had from a child, promising herself that he would soon want to make love with her again. During the hours she spent with him her conviction was growing that they were matched so well it had to be the start of something that would last. There was no hurry. They had all the time in the world.

But Friday was the day she almost died.

CHAPTER NINE

IT WAS a depressing day from the start. Raining again. Sudden heavy showers that were cold enough for snow coming down from the threatening skies. In the studio office the pace was frantic, with problems in the mail and phones that never stopped ringing.

When she had to be out of the office Clancy left the answer-machine on for Bets, but the jinx followed her. It was a classic example of one-of-those-days, where nothing goes easily. She was running herself ragged and by mid-afternoon she felt like a wet rag.

Work was over for the day, but she had promised to drive into the nearest town to a patisserie that sold special hand-made biscuits her mother had to have when friends came over for coffee on Saturday morning.

Parking was a nightmare. The Christmas lights were on and the Christmas shoppers were out. When Clancy had managed to find a space in a backstreet she hurried to get to the shop, and was waiting on the edge of the pavement for the crossing lights to change.

Traffic was streaming by and shoppers were milling all around when a hand or an elbow or a lurching body sent Clancy spinning, hands flailing as they had when she'd been drowning, pitching forward and convulsively twisting herself back. The car whose wheels she should have been under swerved, a second miracle avoiding a pile-up, and Clancy was being dragged up from the gutter to a babel of shouting voices

She was in no pain, so she could not have been injured, and her instinctive reaction was to get away. She heard herself crying, 'I'm all right, I'm okay,' pushing her way through the crowds, oblivious to what they were saying.

She almost ran, head down, keeping close to the walls and windows, like an animal afraid to break cover, until she reached the side street where she had left her car.

She couldn't go to Fergus, he was away for the weekend, and she sat in her car, hands on the wheel, stupefied with shock. She was not fit to drive but she went through the route automatically, negotiating the traffic flow, driving steadily until she reached her home.

Her mother called, 'That you, darling? Did you get my biscuits?' and Clancy tried to call back but could only raise a croak as Esta came into the hall. One look at Clancy and her mother rushed at her, as if she expected her daughter to fall and had to be there to catch her.

The hugging hurt, making Clancy aware of her bruises, but the anguish in Esta's face showed plainer than words how much Clancy meant to her. 'What's happened to you?' Her mother's eyes were full of tears. 'Oh, my baby, what happened?'

Clancy's pale beige raincoat was filthy with mud, and when it fell open her tights were torn and her knees were scratched and bleeding. Her make-up was smudged, her hair dishevelled, and she realised that she must look like a woman who had been assaulted, raped.

She said, 'I was in an accident. Nearly in an accident. I'd been rushing around all day and I had a dizzy spell and fell. That's all.'

Esta, who had just had a nightmare vision of what might have happened, gave a gasp of relief, but the relief did not lessen her concern. Clancy was enveloped in tender care as Esta took off her coat, peeled off the ruined tights and gently bathed the grazed knees. 'Where were you when you fell?' she asked.

'On the crossing by the delicatessen,' Clancy said. Esta went pale, and Clancy wished she had not told her and tried to start sounding better than she felt.

The phone rang while Esta was boiling a kettle for hot sweet tea and Clancy, cleaned up by now and sitting quietly, answered. She had been almost sure it would be Fergus, and when she heard his voice it was a prayer being answered.

He said, 'I'm just leaving. Everything all right?' And, when she hesitated, 'What's up?'

'Can I see you before you go? I'm at home.'

'I'll be there.'

She told her mother, 'Fergus is coming for me,' and Esta sighed but said nothing.

She went outside with Clancy when his car drew up and told him, 'She's had a fall. She fainted, and she's still very shaky.'

'I'm fine now,' Clancy said brightly. He opened the passenger door for her and she got in, smiling to hide the grimace of pain because by now her back was aching and she knew where the worst of the bruises would be.

'What happened to you?' he asked as they came out of the driveway.

'I nearly fell under a car.' She felt him stiffen beside her, but she kept looking ahead. 'I told my mother I felt faint. I was in a crowd, and it had to be an accident, only things have been happening this week, and it might sound paranoid but I can't help wondering if I was knocked into the road.'

He said nothing until he could stop the car. Then he turned towards her. 'Hugh?' he said curtly, and she was utterly incredulous.

'Of *course* not! *Angela!*'

'And what has Angela been doing to give you a persecution complex?'

She told him: the wreath, the weedkiller, the threats that Clancy had no future, phone calls that were heavy breathing with recall blocked. Ending with, 'And she's still at the hotel.'

'Why didn't you tell me about this?'

'Because she wanted you told and me running round like a headless chicken.'

'I don't give a damn what she wants. You should have told me.'

'Well, I'm telling you now.' Her aches were making her irritable. 'I didn't want to be a nuisance, but if push is coming to shove I could use some support.'

'You couldn't be a nuisance. What are friends for?' He put out a hand to stroke her face, and she wanted to press his fingers against her lips, making the touch lover-like. But she sat still and he said, 'The childish tricks are Angela, all right, and I'll put a stop to them, but she hasn't the nerve to be lethal. That has to have been an accident, and thank God it was no worse.'

She shivered, and he said gently, 'You should be taking it easy. Shall I take you home?'

'Where are you going?'

'To send Angela on her way, dead or alive.'

'This I have to see.'

Of course it had been an accident. She had to have imagined the hand in the small of her back, deliberately pitching her towards the crushing wheels.

They walked into the hotel and Sara came from behind the reception desk. Clancy had phoned yesterday, when Sara had told her Angela was still here. There hadn't been any trouble had there? she had asked. 'Nothing to bother about,' Clancy had said.

But now, when Fergus asked, 'Is she in?' Sara knew something was wrong. He had a face that gave nothing away, but Clancy didn't look right. Sara would have asked Clancy what was happening, but she could never have questioned him.

She said, 'She's just come back. I think she's in her room.'

The bedroom door opened. Angela was putting that long blonde fur coat in the wardrobe and she dropped coat and hanger when she saw them. Fergus walked across to her. 'Look at me,' he said. She looked at him, then turned quickly away, and he repeated, 'I said, look at me.'

Slowly her head jerked round, like a puppet on a string, until she was facing him, and what she saw in his eyes drained the colour from her cheeks and made her own eyes dark and fearful. 'I don't understand,' she said in the little-girl voice.

Fergus said softly, slowly, 'Understand this. If anyone harmed Clancy in any way, by word or deed or any nasty little scheme that might crawl into their head, there would be nowhere they could hide from me. I would find them, and when I did they would bitterly regret ever having been born.'

She whispered, 'I don't understand,' again.

'You understand,' he said. 'And you had better believe me.'

She believed him, and so did Clancy. The warning could not have been deadlier if he had held a loaded gun. Clancy had no more to fear from Angela.

It had been an ordeal this week, wondering what she might do next, and Clancy was feeling much happier when they drove away from the hotel, leaving Angela packing her bags. Now Fergus was taking Clancy home again, before setting off for London, while Clancy, bruised and battered from her accident, would spend a quiet evening and hope for a restful night's sleep. On impulse she said, 'Take me to the mill house. I don't want any more fussing and I'd quite like to be alone.'

She would have liked him with her, but he had business meetings with publishers and would be back tomorrow afternoon. She said she was sure she would be fine, and he left her making herself a cheese and pickle sandwich.

She ate that slowly, feeling queasy. By now all her muscles seemed to be stiffening, and she couldn't decide whether to undress and check how bad the bruises were or if she should just lie here on the sofa for another hour or two.

She was dozing when the knocking woke her, and she staggered, slightly disorientated, to the door to let Fergus in. First the rain came at her; it was chucking it down again. Then, as she wiped her eyes, she saw Hugh standing there, not Fergus, and remembered that Fergus would have had a key. The surprise made her sway, clutching the door to steady herself, shocking Hugh, who gasped, 'My God, you are in a bad way.'

She was shaking and aching, far from her usual self,

and the last man she wanted here was Hugh, who came in damp from the downpour, looking flustered and agitated. He said, 'Your mother rang me.'

'So what else is new?' she said wearily. While Fergus had been here she had rung her mother to say where she was, that she was resting. But of course Esta would have to put Hugh in the picture. She said, 'I had a little fall.'

'Your mother said you fainted.'

'I am all right. I only need to rest.'

'He's left you on your own. You need to come home.'

She was too stiff to be nimble, so that Hugh had his arms round her before she could back off, and she howled, 'Don't touch me. I've pulled some muscles.' She reached the sofa and lowered herself down. Hugh followed and sat down beside her, and went on about her coming home while she closed her eyes and tried to shut him out.

She did say, 'Please shut up, please go,' but that didn't even check his voice, which was boring into her temples like a drill. Now he was saying, 'I want to look after you. I'll always look after you. When McKenzie has gone you'll get over this infatuation.'

Her head was throbbing, she was on the verge of hysteria, and she turned on Hugh with a fierce passion. 'No, I will not get over it,' she said. 'Because this is not infatuation. I love Fergus and I shall go on loving him. When he goes away—and he will go; I know that—I shan't be needing anyone else. I shall be waiting for him, and one day I shall be following him. I'd follow him barefoot round the world if I had to. I'd do anything to keep him wanting me, just me and no other woman.'

Hugh had aged as she spoke. When she was silent he looked defeated. Then he said, 'You're killing me.' He stood up slowly, like an old man, and she hardly recognised his voice. 'Why should I want to go on living?' She tried to speak, but this stranger was saying, 'Well, I know what to do now.'

He went out into the rain, leaving the door ajar, and she was terrified for him. She couldn't matter that much to him, but what else could he have meant? She screamed his name and ran after him. In the lights from the house she saw him ahead of her, walking towards the bridge and the turning wheel, and screamed again, 'Hugh, wait!'

She caught up with him on the bridge, with the water churning below, and grabbed his arm. He grinned down at her. 'Come to say goodbye?'

'What are you *doing*?'

He was holding her now, gripping her upper arms. 'I loved you,' he said. 'It would have been all right.'

'Come away from here.'

'This isn't my fault.' The face above hers was grotesque, teeth bared, eyes glaring, but she was completely unprepared when suddenly he was thrusting her backwards, head and shoulders over the wall of the bridge, the rain lashing her face as though the waters were already closing over her.

She was drowning again, struggling in blind terror, fighting for her life while lights were flashing and bursting in her eyes and a high-pitched screaming went on. Like a siren. Or a car hooting. Until she was tumbling back onto the bridge as Hugh's hands fell away from her.

He was gasping for breath, panting, 'I was taking you with me.'

She would never believe this betrayal, not from Hugh. But she said, with a certainty that was breaking her heart, 'No, you were not.' She waited for Fergus, who was running towards them, and as he reached Hugh she said, 'Let him go.'

Fergus snarled, 'It's finished. You're through,' passing Hugh and going down on his knees beside Clancy, who was slumped on the ground. As his arms encircled her she pressed her face into his shoulder, shaking with muffled sobs.

'He knew I'd follow him out here. He tried to kill me. Hugh meant to kill me. I'm going mad; the world's gone mad.'

'Hush.' Fergus was carrying her. 'Hush.'

In the house he laid her gently on the sofa, but everything was whirling around her. She was pounded by waves that could still drown her. She clung to him and reached to clutch the dog's fur, as if they could pull her ashore as they had from the flooded river.

In her weakened state the cold would have crippled her. If she had made it to the bank and tried to climb out Hugh would have kept pushing her back. She would have been sucked under, swept beneath the wheel, if Fergus had not been on the bridge.

She had to keep her eyes on him and listen to every word, because he was her lifeline to sanity in a world gone mad. His voice was calm, steadying her as she listened, in spite of what he was saying. 'I was thinking about your accident. How it could have been Angela behind you in the crowed, acting on impulse. She won't come near again, but then I thought, Who else would feel safer with you out of the way? Hugh Marshall's offices are in town; he could have been on that pavement. He was still here and I'd left you alone.

I turned back, calling myself a fool but knowing I had to stay with you or take you with me.'

The man she had idolised from a child wanted her dead, and her mind splintered in a terrible confusion. 'All these years I thought he cared for me.'

Fergus said quietly, 'He did. In his fashion he still does. But he believes everybody owes him the lifestyle he wants. He's never been brought to book before, but there are enough discrepancies to interest the Fraud Squad, get him struck off and probably sent down. He might not realise how much I know, I doubt if he does, but he knew that if we stayed together I'd be watching your interests and an exposé wouldn't be far off. If nobody sounded the alarm he might have gone on robbing Peter to pay Paul for a few more years.'

'So he planned to murder me.' She should have been screaming, but the words came out in hushed tones.

'I don't think it was a plan,' Fergus said. 'Just a way out that was handed to him. Even if the accident *was* an accident he might have thought it meant you'd fainted once today and were still unsteady. If nobody knew he'd come out here, who could prove you hadn't gone outside and blacked out near the water? Another accident. Perhaps he finally accepted that you were never going back to him.'

This time Hugh had believed her. When the stranger had said, 'You're killing me,' he had meant that Clancy had just signed her own death warrant. The pieces were falling into place like a horrible jigsaw. Losing her daughter might have broken Esta Lindhurst, but it would have made her even more trusting and dependent on the man she looked on as a son.

But Clancy was not in the river under the wheel. She was alive, with the man she loved. 'You saved my life,' she said, and somehow she nearly smiled. 'Again,' she said. 'You're looking after me like the old Chinese proverb says.'

Fergus did smile. 'Never mind the old proverb. I'm keeping you safe because if I lost you I'd have no life.'

'You don't mean that.' He was saying it to make her smile.

He said, 'I mean it as I meant what I told Angela. I am going to marry you.'

'That was a hoax.'

'That was a commitment.' She was still confused, she might be hearing what she wanted to hear. She sat still and listened carefully. He said, 'All right, we've only known each other a few weeks, and you had years believing you were in love with Hugh.' With Hugh she had been in love with love, nothing like the absolute conviction of her feelings for Fergus... 'I was giving you time,' he said. 'But today there might have been no time at all, so to begin with I am telling you I love you. Will you think about that until you get used to it?'

Thinking about it was like moving out of a dark and frightening place into the sunshine. 'Why did you send me home?' she asked. 'Why didn't you let me stay with you?'

'Make no mistake, I wanted you to stay. But I have trouble keeping my hands off you. Even in the cinema, when you were happy to keep as far away from me as you could, I hated that. I couldn't sit there any longer without reaching out for you. I'll always be reaching for you. I never want to be parted from you.

If you hadn't given me an excuse for following you here I'd have very soon found one. I thought I liked you because you were feisty and fanciable, but when I saw you again that day I knew it was much, much more. I wanted to hold you and never let you go, to make love to you on the bridge, there and then.'

It had been that soon with him and nearly that sudden with her. Her heart had leapt when she saw him again, as if he'd been coming back from a long journey and she had been missing him every hour for years.

He leaned back, looking at her. 'If Hugh Marshall had had a blameless record,' he said, 'I'd still have moved heaven and earth to get you away from him— because how could he be the right one for you when I am?'

He could have been asking a casual question but for the blazing intensity in his eyes, and of course he was the one. If she *had* drowned she thought he could have brought her back to life. She could never lie lifeless in his arms.

'Hold me,' she said, and as he drew her closer warmth from the pressure of his hands and lips flowed through her veins. His caresses were the elixir of life that she drank in through every pore while a rising surge of arousal unleashed her sensuality. When she fumbled with the barrier of clothing he slipped it from her, and from himself, and she loved his deep ribcage, the hard lean stomach. She loved all of him, body and soul. She wanted him deep inside her heart of hearts, and naked, breast to breast, she pressed hungrily against him. He had held desire in check until now, but now he met her every need and beyond in a rapturous celebration of total togetherness.

Tomorrow they would do what had to be done. Hugh had to be stopped from cheating those who trusted him. Whether he used this night to make a run for it or stayed, hoping to bluff it out, he had reached the end of the line. Clancy's mother would need all their support when she had to accept that the golden boy had feet of clay. Others would be disbelieving, then shocked to the core. Some of them might be heavy losers. It would be a harrowing time, one of the biggest scandals this town had seen.

Financially Clancy was among the losers, but she was immeasurably rich in everything she needed for a wonderful life. And she counted herself the luckiest of women as all night long she and Fergus held each other in comfort and love.

When the first signs of dawn were streaking the skies he looked down at her as she lay beside him. Her face shimmered in the pale light, sensuous and fulfilled and more beautiful than ever. He said huskily, 'My woman, my wife.' And she liked the sound of both. 'You can have no idea how I feel about you.'

She reached to lace her fingers in his hair and bring his face down so that her smiling lips brushed his. 'Oh, but I have, my love,' she said.

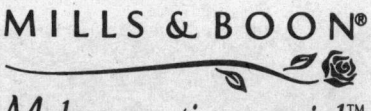

Makes any time special™

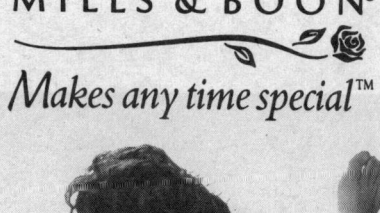

Mills & Boon publish 29 new titles every month. Select from...

Modern Romance™   Tender Romance™

Sensual Romance™

Medical Romance™   Historical Romance™

MAT2

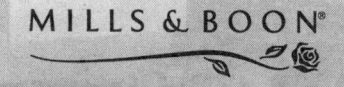
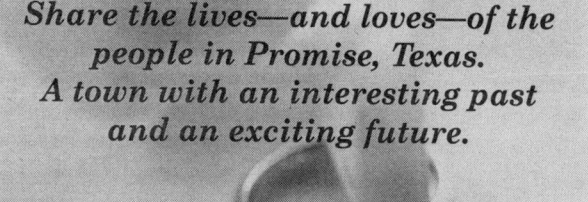

and a surprise gift!

We would like to take this opportunity to thank you for reading this Mills & Boon® book by offering you the chance to take TWO more specially selected titles from the Tender Romance™ series absolutely FREE! We're also making this offer to introduce you to the benefits of the Reader Service™ —

- ★ FREE home delivery
- ★ FREE gifts and competitions
- ★ FREE monthly Newsletter
- ★ Books available before they're in the shops
- ★ Exclusive Reader Service discounts

Accepting these FREE books and gift places you under no obligation to buy; you may cancel at any time, even after receiving your free shipment. Simply complete your details below and return the entire page to the address below. *You don't even need a stamp!*

YES! Please send me 2 free Tender Romance books and a surprise gift. I understand that unless you hear from me, I will receive 4 superb new titles every month for just £2.40 each, postage and packing free. I am under no obligation to purchase any books and may cancel my subscription at any time. The free books and gift will be mine to keep in any case.

N0ZEB

Ms/Mrs/Miss/Mr ....Initials.............................

BLOCK CAPITALS PLEASE

Surname..

Address...

....

....Postcode ....

Send this whole page to:
UK: The Reader Service, FREEPOST CN81, Croydon, CR9 3WZ
EIRE: The Reader Service, PO Box 4546, Kilcock, County Kildare (stamp required)